I really have found my soul mate, Elizabeth thought as Ben Morgan leaned forward, his warm lips sending shivers up her spine.

Suddenly the moon and stars were swallowed up in a flood of light that washed over the deck. Elizabeth staggered backward, almost blinded by the white-hot lights from just off starboard.

"What the—" Ben began in a surprisingly harsh voice.

"Drop your weapon and put your hands up!" a voice boomed through a loudspeaker.

Elizabeth shook her head. "You've made a mistake!" she screamed toward the boat that had pulled alongside. Then Ben pulled her toward him, and Elizabeth's mouth dropped open.

A huge knife glinted in his hand.

Elizabeth looked up into the eyes of her soul mate, and all she saw was hatred.

A STRANGER
IN THE HOUSE

Written by
Kate William

Created by
FRANCINE PASCAL

BANTAM BOOKS
NEW YORK • TORONTO • LONDON • SYDNEY • AUCKLAND

RL 6, age 12 and up

A STRANGER IN THE HOUSE
A Bantam Book / July 1995

Sweet Valley High® *is a registered trademark of Francine Pascal*
Conceived by Francine Pascal
Produced by Daniel Weiss Associates, Inc.
33 West 17th Street
New York, NY 10011
Cover art by Bruce Emmett

ISBN: 0-553-56711-X

Published simultaneously in the United States and Canada

Bantam Books are published by Bantam Books, a division of Bantam
Doubleday Dell Publishing Group, Inc. Its trademark, consisting of the
words "Bantam Books" and the portrayal of a rooster, is Registered in
U.S. Patent and Trademark Office and in other countries. Marca
Registrada. Bantam Books, 1540 Broadway, New York, New York 10036.

PRINTED IN THE UNITED STATES OF AMERICA

OPM   0 9 8 7 6 5 4 3 2 1

To Molly Jessica W. Wenk

Prologue

Scissor blades gleamed, slicing through newsprint. The sports section of the *Sweet Valley News* fell away and floated to the cement floor, a rectangular window cut from its front page. John Marin shoved the forbidden scissors under his mattress. Then he scrutinized the newspaper photo as he thoughtfully stroked his unshaven face.

An eighteen-year-old Sweet Valley man, Nicholas Morrow, had won a local sailing race. Morrow stood on the deck of his boat, grinning for the camera as his trophy shone in the afternoon sunlight.

"Eighteen," Marin muttered, glaring at the young man's handsome, smiling face. "That's just how old I was. . . ." He allowed himself a few seconds to savor the thought of being as free as Morrow to sail on the blue Pacific. He squinted, as if peering into the California sun. He drew a long, deep breath. But the stuffy, slightly rancid odor of the prison cell blocked out all memories of the tang of salt in the air. "It doesn't matter," he told the smiling young man in the photo. "It won't be long now."

But Morrow wasn't the reason John Marin had clipped the photograph. The reason was in the background. The sailboat's crew for the race was a group of local teenagers, two of whom were visible behind Morrow.

A beautiful blond girl was on the right. As she climbed from the rigging a tall, dark-haired guy reached for her hand. The girl's hair was pulled back in a windblown ponytail; her slim legs showed tanned and shapely beneath a pair of loose white shorts. The boy was identified as Todd Wilkins, but it was the girl who interested Marin.

He stared at her face, feeling a familiar rush of hatred. "Elizabeth Wakefield," he whispered, sneering. "Daddy's number-one girl."

Marin taped the newspaper clipping on the wall over his cot, next to a color photograph snipped from the front page of a gossip tabloid a few months earlier.

"And there's Daddy's number-two baby, playing *Lifestyles of the Rich and Famous*," he said, shifting his gaze to the tabloid photo. In this one a radiant, golden-haired teenager in red sequins stood between a rock star and an actor. A man who didn't know any better would have thought the blonde in the tabloid and the girl on the sailboat were one and the same. The long legs, the golden tans, and the heart-shaped faces were identical. But Marin did know better. He had studied the twins for ten long, empty years.

Marin studied Jessica Wakefield's face. A glamorous makeup job complemented the loose, sexy waves of her elaborately tousled blond hair.

"You do love hanging out with the Hollywood crowd, don't you, Jessica?" he asked. "I'm sure I can find a way to make use of that information."

The photo had been taken while the twins guest-starred briefly on a popular soap opera. Marin had watched every one of the twins' episodes, sitting with the other inmates in the crowded common room of the state prison. Normally, watching soaps was an excuse for good-natured ribbing and raunchy comments about actresses. But Marin had demanded silence on the first day of the twins' appearance on *The Young and the Beautiful*. And silence was what he got. Despite Marin's youthful appearance, the other prisoners had learned to comply when he gave an order.

He scanned the other clippings on the cinder-block wall. The twins and their older brother, Steven, beaming at their father, a candidate for town mayor . . . Jessica winning a beauty pageant . . . Elizabeth placing first in an essay contest . . . Elizabeth modeling jungle-print clothes, as part of a promotion to save the rain forest . . . Jessica chosen to appear on a talk show . . . Elizabeth kidnapped and then returned, unharmed . . . Jessica at the wedding of her best friend's parents . . . Elizabeth acquitted of man-slaughter after a boy died in an accident in the Jeep she was driving. . . .

3

"I should have been acquitted too, ten years ago," Marin muttered, glaring again at the girl on the rigging of the sailboat. But finally, that wrong would be righted. He would be as free as Elizabeth and her sister. "It won't be long now," he said again, narrowing his eyes. "Not long at all."

Chapter 1

Elizabeth was halfway through her cereal Monday morning when Jessica skipped into the bright, Spanish-tiled kitchen where the rest of the Wakefield family was eating breakfast.

"No more pencils, no more books! No more teachers' dirty looks!" Jessica sang out. She twirled around in the kitchen, as if she were wearing a tutu instead of khaki shorts and a turquoise polo shirt. Elizabeth was wearing an identical shirt, tucked into her own khaki shorts.

Elizabeth shook her head, amused. Jessica sounded as if she were half the twins' real age, which was sixteen.

Alice Wakefield smiled. "I take it you're happy about the first day of summer vacation, Jess."

"Are you kidding? This is going to be the most awesome summer in the history of the universe."

"Ah, yes," eighteen-year-old Steven Wakefield

said with a nod. "The Golden Age of Greece, the Renaissance, and the Age of Enlightenment will be merely footnotes in history compared to the summer Jessica Wakefield waited tables at the Marina Café."

"Ha!" Jessica retorted. "You're just jealous because you'll be cooped up in a boring old law office while Liz and I are collecting humongous tips and meeting cute guys who surf and own yachts."

Elizabeth grinned at her sister and passed her the milk. "Leave it to you to make serving sandwiches sound glamorous."

"Those are certainly glamorous outfits you're both wearing today," Steven commented, gesturing toward the twins' matching polo shirts. "I thought you two clones gave up dressing alike about ten years ago."

Jessica sliced a banana over her granola. "We did—unless there's something we can get out of impersonating each other, that is. But this is different."

Elizabeth laughed. "You are looking at the official waitress uniform for the Marina Café," she said. "Except for our matching necklaces, of course." She fingered the gold lavaliere she always wore around her neck, identical to Jessica's. "See? The shirts have the café's logo on them. They come directly from fashion runways of Milan and Paris."

"I think she means *airport* runways," Jessica said. "I feel like a baggage handler. Khakis aren't exactly the height of chic."

"I *like* khakis!" Elizabeth protested.

"You would." Jessica shrugged, holding a glass of cranberry juice in her hand. A few ruby droplets

6

spattered the smooth white tablecloth. "You're such a prep, Liz. I'm just glad Mr. Jenkins said we could wear shorts. And the turquoise shirt *does* match our eyes."

"That's a relief!" Steven said. "You wouldn't want your clothes to clash with your eyes. What would people say?"

"I see that you've been taking sarcasm lessons from Elizabeth. And fashion lessons from Dad." Jessica pointed her spoon at her brother's gray suit and then at their father's. The similarity was emphasized by the fact that Ned Wakefield looked like an older version of his brown-eyed, dark-haired son. Ned sat across the table from Jessica, but he was engrossed in the morning newspaper and apparently hadn't heard a word of the conversation. Jessica shook her head in an exaggerated way. "Steven, you're dressed like you're about forty years old."

Mrs. Wakefield smiled. "I think you look quite handsome, Steven."

"You have to say that," Jessica pointed out. "You're his mother."

Elizabeth rolled her eyes. Jessica and Steven were capable of teasing back and forth all day.

"But I suppose you have to wear dull clothes if you're going to fit in at a stuffy law firm," Jessica continued. "You'd never catch me wasting a perfectly good summer doing something so *serious*."

Elizabeth shook her head. "Only you can make 'serious' sound like a disease."

"It *is* a disease."

"I happen to be excited about being an intern in Dad's office," Steven announced. "Law offices don't generally take in undergraduates."

"So why did they hire you?" Jessica asked. "Was it your overwhelming brainpower, your sterling resume, or the fact that Dad's a partner in the firm?"

"Tell her, Dad," Steven urged. "Tell her about my brilliant interview with Marianna West and the other partners."

Ned Wakefield looked up, startled, from the *Sweet Valley News.* "Sorry, Steven," he said with a weak smile. "I guess I wasn't paying attention. What were you saying?"

"That's certainly a glowing endorsement," Jessica said through a mouthful of granola. "I hope you held the other partners' attention that well in your interview."

Steven grinned. "When I'm a rich corporate attorney, you just see if I buy you a mansion in Beverly Hills."

Elizabeth sighed. The bickering was lighthearted, but it was getting on her nerves. It was definitely time for a new topic of conversation. "Speaking of mansions, Mom," she began, "you were telling us about the huge house you're working on this summer. How many bedrooms did you say it has?"

"Seven!" Mrs. Wakefield said. "But we're planning to knock out a wall and turn the three front rooms into an enormous master suite."

"It sounds great!"

"The architect I'm working with is based up in

8

Oakland. You should see his sketches, Liz. They're really something. He's managed to do a terrific job, despite the, uh, eccentricities of the house's owner."

Elizabeth laughed. "How eccentric are we talking? Does he want a moat around the place?"

"Not quite. But get this—in the master bathroom, the client insists on having a fireplace!"

"Cool!" Jessica exclaimed. "Can Liz and I put a fireplace in our bathroom?"

"I don't think so, Jessica." Mrs. Wakefield smiled.

Elizabeth drank the last of her cranberry juice. "So, Mom, what kind of decorating theme do you think you'll go with?"

"I've decided on a southwestern motif," Mrs. Wakefield told her. "It's a little trendier than I usually do, but the desert colors will be great with the simple lines of the architecture."

"Should be nice," Jessica said, suddenly sounding distracted. Elizabeth followed her twin's gaze to the back page of Mr. Wakefield's newspaper. A colorful ad announced the annual Summer Fun sale at Valley Mall. No doubt Jessica would spend her first week's waitressing tips before she'd even earned them.

Mr. Wakefield turned the page and refolded the paper. Jessica sighed and picked up her bagel.

"I'm keeping all the walls white," Mrs. Wakefield continued, "with accents in a muted coral tone—"

She stopped as Mr. Wakefield began choking on his toast.

"What is it, Dad?" Elizabeth asked.

9

Jessica raised her eyebrows. "I don't think he likes muted coral."

"Ned, are you all right? Do you want some water?"

"I'm fine," he insisted after a moment. "Everything's OK. Nothing's wrong at all."

Elizabeth and her mother exchanged a concerned look. Elizabeth glanced back at her father, but his eyes were riveted to the newspaper. He had regained his composure, but Ned Wakefield's face was as white as the tablecloth.

Mr. Wakefield took a deep breath and tried to pretend nothing was wrong. *In all likelihood,* he told himself, *there really is nothing wrong.* He was probably overreacting to the short item he'd spotted in the *Sweet Valley News.* Of course he was overreacting.

He reread the headline: PAROLE BOARD GRANTS FIFTEEN-YEAR REPRIEVE. The message was there in black and white, but Ned couldn't believe it.

Around the courthouse Ned Wakefield had a reputation for progressive views on rehabilitation. But even he was convinced that some criminals were unsalvageable. He had learned that lesson more than ten years ago, when he was a young assistant district attorney.

He held the newspaper in front of his face and closed his eyes for a few seconds, remembering. . . .

The jury members' horrified gasps were audible when Ned passed around the crime-scene photo-

10

graphs of the golden-haired college student and her mother. The two women had driven to Secca Lake for a picnic on a sunny June day. They'd been abducted and held in a cabin a few miles away. A week later the kidnapper dumped the bodies in the woods, stabbed a dozen times each.

There was no doubt in Ned's mind that the defendant was guilty. And only a monster could have murdered those two lovely, innocent women, even though their family had paid the exorbitant ransom he'd demanded. A man who had committed such a crime deserved to be locked up forever. . . .

Ned had thought he'd presented an airtight case. But then the defendant took the stand and almost talked his way out of a conviction—despite the fact that every bit of evidence proved he was the murderer. This guy had been slick, all right, with his baby face and innocent eyes. By the time the defendant stepped down from the witness stand, the jury was like putty in his strong, lethal hands. Ned could see it in their eyes: those twelve citizens were set to find the monster innocent. It was up to Ned to change their minds.

"A case rests on facts, not on personalities or appearances," Ned reminded the jury. "Forget the slick talk. Forget the neat haircut and the pressed suit. The defendant brutally murdered two innocent women." He paused to emphasize that point.

"You, the jury, are obligated to the truth. And the truth is that this man"—Ned gestured toward the defendant—"is guilty, beyond any reasonable

*doubt. You've seen the police reports. You've heard
the testimony and reviewed the evidence. You know
that the defendant's alibi fell apart under questioning. You know that the victims' blood was found on
his clothes and hands. And you saw the photographs of the bodies of two women whose only mistake was to choose the wrong afternoon for a picnic
at Secca Lake."*

Ten years later Ned shook his head behind the
newspaper, remembering the horror of the crime.
Those two women had been slaughtered, pure and
simple. And he had never wanted to win a case so
badly, before or since. Few trials seemed to hit home
with Ned the way that one had. The lake was a popular
spot. His own young family often picnicked there; the
jurors probably spent time at Secca Lake with their
own families as well. He wanted them to realize—to
understand deep down—that the murdered women
could have just as easily been their own wives or
daughters or sisters.

Ned had felt no happiness at the guilty verdict—
only relief. The twenty-five-year sentence wasn't the
life term he'd hoped for, but it had seemed like
enough to keep the killer off the streets for a good,
long time.

Now, only ten years later, John Marin was free on
parole. And the police had never recovered the ransom money, so he was probably a rich man.

Surely money and freedom would be enough for
Marin. He must have forgotten the threats he'd made

that day, as the police pulled him to his feet and began leading him out of the courtroom. . . .

Handcuffs clanked as the murderer shrugged away from the officers and leaned over the prosecutor's table. "I'll get you, Wakefield," he hissed into Ned's ear. "And you can be sure I'll hit you where you live." Ned felt the color drain from his face.

The convicted man struggled against the officers, who jerked him toward the exit. "How are those three perfect children of yours, Counselor?" Marin called in a menacing tone. "I won't forget you, Wakefield!" Marin shouted back over his shoulder as they led him down the aisle. "Your precious little girls will never be safe again!"

Ned turned to watch John Marin's back retreating out the door of the courtroom. But all he could see were the chubby faces of an eight-year-old boy and two golden-haired girls—the prettiest six-year-olds in the first-grade class.

"Yo! Earth to Dad!" Jessica called to her father. She kissed him on the cheek and was amused when he jumped. "Boy, were you ever zoning!"

"What's the matter, Dad?" Elizabeth asked, pecking him on the other cheek.

"Not a thing," he said quickly, giving them a tight smile. "I'm just a little tired. But are you girls really sure you want to take jobs this summer? I mean, you won't have many carefree summers left before college and work. Maybe you should consider just staying close to home for the next few months."

"Sounds good to me," Jessica said. "If you'd consider tripling my allowance!"

"I thought you said working at the café would be good experience," Elizabeth said. "You know, teach us responsibility and all that."

Leave it to Liz to think about responsibility, Jessica thought.

"Yeah, Dad," Steven said. "I thought it was you who suggested summer jobs in the first place."

Mrs. Wakefield placed a hand on her husband's arm. "Why the cold feet all of a sudden?"

Mr. Wakefield smiled. "I guess I'm just becoming sentimental in my old age, seeing my baby daughters grown up enough to have jobs."

"Come on, Jess," Elizabeth urged. "We won't have jobs much longer if we're late to work on our first day."

Jessica drained her glass of cranberry juice. "Punctuality is next to godliness, you know," she confided to Steven in her best Elizabeth voice.

"That's cleanliness," her mother reminded her. "As in, remember that you promised to vacuum the living room by tonight. Time's running out."

Jessica sighed. She'd been hoping her mother had forgotten that promise. Vacuuming wasn't the kind of thing Jessica generally offered to do. But she'd made the promise in a weak moment, when she desperately needed an advance on her allowance to buy a cool pair of bright red sandals. "It would really make more sense to have Elizabeth do the living room," she tried. "She does a much better job of vacuuming than I do—"

"Save your breath!" Elizabeth interrupted. "I'm busy tonight." She turned to her parents. "I forgot to mention that I won't be home for dinner. I'm going out with Todd."

Mr. Wakefield stared at her, his brown eyes intense. "Be home early." Slowly he stood and walked to the window. "And I want both of you girls to be careful today," he said quietly. "Don't talk to strangers."

In the doorway Jessica grunted and rolled her eyes. "Sure thing, Dad. We'll just ask for people's orders in sign language."

Mr. Wakefield watched the twins breeze out the door. He froze when he felt a hand on his shoulder.

"Is something wrong, Ned?" Alice asked. "You seem preoccupied."

"No, no," he said, making an effort to disguise the tension in his voice. "It's just like I said—I'm a little tired. I haven't been getting enough sleep, thanks to this wrongful-dismissal suit—"

"You have been working awfully long hours, Dad," Steven said. "But never fear. Starting today, you'll have *me* in the office to help you out. Maybe you'll be able to come home a little earlier."

"Spending more time at home isn't such a bad idea," Mr. Wakefield said thoughtfully. He turned back to the window to watch the girls in the driveway

15

as they argued about who was going to drive the black Jeep Wrangler they shared.

"I won't forget you, Wakefield," Marin had said. But surely, after ten years . . .

"Dammit," Mr. Wakefield swore under his breath. How could the parole board be so blind? John Marin was a dangerous criminal. And now he was free.

"He's probably forgotten all about me," he whispered to the windowpane, trying to believe it. His heart filled with love for his children.

Behind him laughter rang out, cheerful and carefree. Steven was joking with Alice as they loaded the breakfast plates into the dishwasher. Outside, the girls had resolved their argument over driving rights—as usual, by Elizabeth giving in to her more headstrong twin. Jessica glided into the driver's seat while Elizabeth climbed in on the other side. Both twins were smiling as Jessica gunned the engine.

The Jeep moved away, growing smaller in the distance. And Mr. Wakefield felt a torrent of fear as his daughters sped out of his sight.

Chapter 2

"Dad was a major space cadet this morning," Jessica commented as she steered the Jeep toward the marina.

"He did seem kind of weird," Elizabeth admitted. She rolled down her window to feel closer to the bright blue sky and the white-gold sunlight that danced on the well-kept lawns of Calico Drive. Despite the beautiful June day, Elizabeth felt troubled by her father's uncharacteristic anxiety. "What do you think is wrong with him?"

"He said something about a tough case his firm is handling, going up against some big-time corporation. Maybe he's afraid he's going to lose."

"I suppose that could be it. Or maybe it's like he says. He's just tired."

Jessica grinned. "Or he's been abducted by aliens and replaced with a Martian clone."

"I'm sure he'll be normal by tonight," Elizabeth

said, hoping it was true. "He's been so excited about having Steven in the office with him. I bet their first day of working together will make him feel more like himself."

"Well, I'm sure looking forward to *our* first day of work," Jessica said.

Elizabeth nodded. "Me too. Waitressing isn't the most intellectually stimulating summer job I might have hoped for, but it's going to be fun."

Jessica snorted. "Intellectual? Leave it to you to even suggest that a summer job should be intellectual. Think about it, Liz. We're spending the whole summer at the marina! Sunny days, huge tips, guys with yachts—"

"Heavy trays to carry, vegetables to slice, rude customers—"

"Don't be so pessimistic, Elizabeth. Just take it from me—this is going to be the most perfect summer ever."

Elizabeth shrugged. "And *you* take it from *me*— waitressing is hard work. We'll be right near the beach, but it's not as though we're spending the summer lying on a towel, scoping guys—like somebody else we know."

Jessica batted her eyelashes. "Why, whoever could you mean?" she said in a bad imitation of a southern accent.

"You know who I mean," Elizabeth said, thinking of Jessica's wealthy but spoiled best friend. "The only thing Lila Fowler's planning to work at this summer is her tan."

"But at least she'll be nearby. She can come into the café every day with reports on good-looking surfers—and spend some of her millions on big tips for me."

"Enid will be close by too," Elizabeth said, referring to her own best friend. "Did I tell you she got the lifeguard job she was after? She just called me last night with the news."

"What a waste," Jessica said. "You can see that high platform from every part of the beach—and sitting on it will be Enid Rollins, the World's Most Boring Teenager. There really ought to be a law: Lifeguards should all be hot guys with big biceps and washboard stomachs."

"I didn't think you'd be mooning over cute lifeguards this summer, Jess. What about Ken Matthews? Just because he's out of town for the month, do you plan to forget that you have a steady boyfriend now?"

"I'll miss Ken," Jessica said with a shrug. "But what can I do about it? His parents decided to take the family to Monterey to visit his uncle Frank. So I'll just have to have a good time without him."

"I thought you were in love!"

"I am. But I'm sure Ken doesn't expect me to mope around for a month alone. He wants me to have a good time while he's gone. It's like that song from when Mom and Dad were young—love the one you're with!"

"I can't believe he really meant *that*."

"Maybe not exactly. But how would *you* know?

You and boring old Todd don't understand the first thing about having fun."

"Todd's not boring—" Elizabeth began loyally, defending her longtime boyfriend, Todd Wilkins.

"Of course, Todd *is* a hunk," Jessica admitted, interrupting her. "It's his only redeeming quality. But you've been dating him for a million years!"

"That's why I'm so glad he'll be working at the marina too," Elizabeth said. "I like having him close by."

Jessica shook her head in disgust. "Exactly. And you'll probably still see him every single day, when he comes into the café between windsurfing lessons."

"What's wrong with seeing my boyfriend every day?"

Jessica shrugged. "Nothing, I guess. But it's not just your boring relationship with Todd. Face the truth. You're in serious danger, Liz. And you don't even know it."

"What are you talking about?"

"You're in danger of growing up into a nerd! You're boring! You need to take more risks in life. Do something wild and crazy for a change."

"That's ridiculous," Elizabeth protested. But she felt interested in spite of herself. "Like what?"

"Have a secret romance. Rob a bank. Take up bungee jumping. You know, get a life!"

"I have a life!" Elizabeth protested. "A very nice life." Too late, she realized how weak that sounded. As a writer, she was sure that her thesaurus omitted

"nice" when listing synonyms for "wild and crazy."
She started again, trying to be completely honest. "I
have a very interesting, active, fulfilling life."

"Right," Jessica said, rolling her eyes. "Name me
one single night in the last two weeks that you've
done anything the least bit fun."

Elizabeth opened her mouth to speak, but then
shut it. She *had* been working awfully hard, studying
for final exams and writing several articles for the
year-end edition of the *Oracle,* the student newspaper at Sweet Valley High. "Well," she said finally,
"Todd and I stopped at the Dairi Burger after school
Friday for a celebration milk shake."

"You party animal!"

Elizabeth sighed. "I give up! You're absolutely
right. I'm a drone."

Jessica's mouth dropped open. "I'm *right*? You
mean you're agreeing with me? Call the news-
papers!"

"The truth is, I've sort of been reevaluating my
life for the past few weeks," Elizabeth admitted.

"Then why were you arguing with me?"

"I guess I didn't realize exactly what was wrong
until now. I can finally see that I'm in a serious rut. I
do a lot of things that are fun. But I've been doing
the *same* fun things over and over again, all year
long!"

Jessica pulled the Jeep to a stop at a red light and
turned to face her sister. "So you admit you're in a
rut. That's the first step toward becoming a recover-
ing dullaholic. The next step is to find a way to shake

yourself out of this dismal pattern. Might I suggest skydiving?"

"Don't press your luck."

Elizabeth thought for a minute as Jessica drove through the intersection and turned down the driveway that led to the marina. "You know, Jessica, I always claim I want to be a writer when I grow up. But how will I ever think of anything to write about if I haven't *experienced* life?"

"Exactly! Didn't Mr. Collins say that Hemingway hung out in bars all the time? And that Edgar Allan Poe was a real partyer? They didn't spend their whole lives sitting behind a computer monitor, typing."

Elizabeth grinned. "They couldn't have if they wanted to. Word processors hadn't been invented yet."

"You know what I mean."

Elizabeth nodded. "Yes, I guess I do." Roger Collins, her favorite teacher, was always telling fascinating stories about authors' lives. And none of the stories included anecdotes about weekends spent studying for exams. Elizabeth took a deep breath. "I still need to work out the details, but my mind's made up," she announced. "Somehow I'm going to find a way to have a summer full of adventure, risk, and life experiences!"

Jessica pulled the Jeep to a stop in the parking lot at the marina. Then she turned and grinned at her sister. "You know what, Lizzie? There may be hope for you yet."

°   °   °

"Ah, the twins!" exclaimed Mr. Jenkins, the owner of the marina café, as Jessica and Elizabeth walked in. He stroked his mustache and stepped out from behind the counter that ran along the back wall of the dining room. "I hope my new waitresses are ready for a busy day."

Jessica smiled brightly. "Hi, Mr. Jenkins!" She glanced at her sister, remembering Elizabeth's resolve to seek out excitement this summer. "I think both of us are ready for just about anything."

"That's great, Elizabeth!" Mr. Jenkins said, smiling at Jessica. "Enthusiasm is one of the most important traits of a good waitress."

"Actually, I'm Jessica. She's Liz."

Mr. Jenkins scratched his nearly bald head. "Jessica? Goodness, and I thought I finally had it straight by the end of your interview last week. Well, I'm sure I'll remember from now on."

"The café opens at nine thirty, right?" Elizabeth asked. "It's almost eight forty-five now. Do you want us to jump right in and get to work? We can start getting food out, or make sure all the tables have napkins and silverware—"

Mr. Jenkins smiled broadly at Elizabeth. "It's refreshing to see a girl your age with such a sense of responsibility, Jessica."

Jessica rolled her eyes. Elizabeth's efforts to be wild and crazy this summer were definitely off to a slow start.

Mr. Jenkins checked his watch. "We'll have you both hard at work soon enough. But first, I'd like to spend a half hour on orientation for you and two other new waitresses. We'll begin in a few minutes. You can wait for me in the storage room."

"Where's that?" Jessica asked as he began to bustle away.

"Oh. See the two doors behind the counter? The one on the right leads to the kitchen. The other is to the storage room. I'll join you in there shortly."

Morning sunlight coming through the window behind Ned Wakefield cast a shadow on the folded newspaper that lay on his mahogany desk at the law office. Marianna West, another partner in the firm, sat across from him, holding a thick stack of file folders.

"Here's what I needed your help on," she said, shoving a stray lock of strawberry blond hair out of her eyes. "It's the *Stone versus West Coast Oilcam* case. You know almost everyone in town, Ned. Can you suggest someone I could call? I need an expert witness who can testify to . . ."

Mr. Wakefield tried to keep his mind on *West Coast Oilcam,* but John Marin's image hovered in front of him like the Ghost of Murders Past. Of course Marin had been bluffing when he threatened revenge against the Wakefield family. Hadn't he?

"Excuse me, Marianna." A new voice penetrated his thoughts and Mr. Wakefield jumped in his seat. But it was only Trudy Roman, the office manager. "Sorry to startle you, Ned. I just wanted to let you know that I haven't been able to locate that old case file you asked for." She consulted her clipboard. "The *Marin* case."

"What do you mean, you can't locate it?" Mr. Wakefield demanded, his voice rising.

Trudy's brown eyes widened. "Sorry, Ned. But it's a ten-year-old case. City hall keeps a lot of the really old files in off-site storage a couple miles outside of town. I'll ask one of the interns to drive over and take a look."

Ned nodded. "Good. Sorry I lost my temper." He smiled weakly. "I didn't sleep much last night."

Trudy smiled. "Don't worry about it. Who would you like me to send after that case file? Your son, Steven?"

"No!" Ned said quickly. The last thing he wanted was for anyone in his family to find out about Marin. There was no need to frighten them until he knew whether or not the man was a real threat. "I mean, it's only Steven's first day. Besides, Phil Bowen has proven to be a real whiz at ferreting out lost information. It, uh, sounds like a good challenge for him."

"I'll get him right on it," Trudy said. She turned to go, but stopped in the doorway. "By the way, I just spoke to Amanda Mason in Sacramento."

"How's her work with the subcommittee going?" Marianna asked. "That was a real coup, having someone from our firm asked to provide legal counsel to the state legislature."

"Amanda's doing well, but she's feeling overwhelmed. She's begging us to send someone to help her out for a few weeks."

Mr. Wakefield wasn't particularly interested in Amanda's personnel problems, but immersing himself in office minutia was probably the best way to keep his mind off Marin—if that was possible. The *Sweet Valley News* on his desk was folded to the story about the murderer's parole, and his eyes kept straying to the headline. He forced them to look up at Trudy instead. "We can't spare another associate right now—not with the *Oilcam* hearing starting in less than a week."

"Oh, Amanda doesn't need an attorney," Trudy said. "The work is routine, even for a paralegal—scheduling meetings, attending briefings, maybe writing an occasional first draft of a report."

Marianna frowned. "It will be hard to convince any of the assistants to go to Sacramento at this time of year. Everyone's kids just got out of school, and people are planning vacations."

Mr. Wakefield's mind was wandering again. He stared at the Marin article, silently cursing the parole board. He prayed again that he was overreacting. But he could still see the cold glint in Marin's eyes as he threatened the Wakefield children. Now he feared the worst. If only there were something—anything—he could do to keep his children safe.

"So what's the solution?" Trudy asked. "Who can we send to Sacramento?"

Mr. Wakefield leaped from his seat. "Steven!"

Marianna laughed. "I haven't seen you this animated all morning, Ned."

Mr. Wakefield felt his face turn pink. But it was

the perfect solution. At least one family member would be out of Marin's reach for a few weeks.

"It's not a bad idea," Trudy said. "It would be great experience for Steven to see the state legislature in action. And he'd be an enormous help to Amanda."

"But Ned," Marianna said. "You were so excited to have Steven home from college for the summer. Are you sure you want to send him four hundred miles away?"

Mr. Wakefield nodded. "Absolutely."

Marianna laughed. "Don't you think you ought to mention it to Steven first?"

Mr. Wakefield forced a smile. "Oh, he'll be thrilled. I can't wait to tell him about it."

"Great," Trudy said. "When should I tell Amanda to expect him?"

Mr. Wakefield slapped his hand down on the newspaper. "Tomorrow morning. Steven will be on the first plane out of town."

He turned and pretended to be interested in the scene outside the window; the sun shone brightly on the colonial-style brick courthouse across the town square. A dachshund picked its way across the emerald lawn, with two blond teenage girls strolling along behind, talking and laughing.

Mr. Wakefield pursed his lips. He had found a way to get Steven to safety. But his daughters were still in Sweet Valley. And so was John Marin.

Chapter 3

Elizabeth's foot was falling asleep. She shifted her weight on the crate of canned hams she was perched on in the storage room of the Marina Café. Luckily Mr. Jenkins seemed to be drawing his orientation session to a close.

"The last thing I want you to remember is that customer service is the key to a successful restaurant," he pronounced, gazing at each of the four new waitresses in turn. "A satisfied customer is a frequent customer. And frequent customers keep us in business."

"Does that mean we have to be nice to people all the time?" Jessica asked. "Even if they're losers?"

Mr. Jenkins's eyebrows rose halfway up his shiny expanse of forehead. "The customer may not always be right, Elizabeth, but the customer is paying the bills—not to mention your tips. So the object is to provide excellent customer service—even to, um, losers."

Elizabeth opened her mouth to say *She's Jessica; I'm Elizabeth,* but Jessica responded first. "So dropping soup on nasty customers would be out of the question?" Jessica's blue-green eyes had a mischievous twinkle.

Mr. Jenkins frowned. "Yes, Elizabeth," he said, hesitating as if he was trying to decide whether or not she was serious. "That would be an inappropriate response."

Elizabeth sighed. Jessica was enjoying this—saying outrageous things and assuming Mr. Jenkins would blame them on Elizabeth. *Oh, well,* she decided, remembering her resolution to be wild and crazy. *I'll just be on the lookout for ways to take advantage of his confusion too. Jessica shouldn't have all the fun.* Elizabeth leaned back against a metal shelving unit piled with stacks of plastic bowls for the salad bar.

"So how do we tell if customers are satisfied?" asked one of the other waitresses, a petite, dark-haired girl about the same age as the twins.

Mr. Jenkins clapped his hands. "The best indicator of excellent service is an excellent tip," he said with a grand gesture. "So I'm sponsoring my annual tip contest for the serving staff."

Elizabeth leaned forward. This sounded interesting.

"Who remembers what I told you about reporting your tips?" Mr. Jenkins asked.

"I didn't know there was going to be a pop quiz," Jessica complained under her breath.

Elizabeth spoke up. "You said we'll each be required to report our tips to you or the manager on duty at the end of each shift."

"Good job, Jessica. I'm glad to know you've been listening so attentively."

Elizabeth grimaced after he turned away. But Jessica was grinning like a jack-o'-lantern.

"For the next week," Mr. Jenkins continued, "I will be tallying that information. For each waitress I'll arrive at the average total tips earned in one shift, between now and Saturday evening. On Saturday the employee with the highest average will win an evening out—including dinner for two at the Box Tree Café, as well as movie passes for Valley Cinema."

"All right!" Jessica cheered loudly, giving a thumbs-up sign.

Mr. Jenkins glared at her for a moment before continuing. "Of course, we want you to be well dressed for your night on the town. So the winner will also receive a fifty-dollar gift certificate for Lisette's Boutique at Valley Mall."

Jessica punched the air with her fist. "Yes!" she yelled.

Mr. Jenkins gave her another long stare. "I hope you show as much enthusiasm for your waitressing work, Elizabeth."

"Oh, yes," Elizabeth responded, with a sidelong glance at Jessica. "Enthusiasm is her middle name."

"Good. Well, that's all you need to know right now. If you find you have questions, feel free to ask me—or Jane O'Reilly, whom you met a few minutes ago."

Elizabeth recalled the tall, red-haired woman in her mid-twenties who had popped into the storage room during their orientation. Elizabeth hadn't had a chance to speak with Jane, but she'd instantly liked her ready smile and warm brown eyes.

"Has Jane been working here a long time?" Elizabeth asked.

"This is Jane's fourth summer at the café," Mr. Jenkins explained. "She knows the job better than anyone."

Jessica pushed a stray strand of hair out of her eyes. She hated to admit it, but Elizabeth had been right, as usual. Waitressing was hard work. She'd been at it for most of the day, with only a short break for lunch with Lila. Her feet ached and her shoulders were sore from carrying the heavy trays of food. But her tips were piling up. After she won the customer-satisfaction contest, she'd take all that hard-earned cash to the Summer Fun sale at Valley Mall. A scarlet miniskirt would be perfect with her new red sandals, and she had seen a cool one at Lisette's.

She sighed and picked up a tray of drinks. Then she marched out into the crowded dining room.

A heavyset man waved impatiently. "Are those our soft drinks?" he demanded. "It's about time." He had greasy-looking hair and a bad sunburn.

"Yes, sir," Jessica assured him, as if bringing him and his family their drinks were the most important thing in the world to her. She smiled broadly, trying to pretend he wasn't a complete jerk. *It's a good thing I have a lot of experience as an actress.*

She served the glasses of milk to two grubby, sand-encrusted children who kept taking swipes at each other.

"We asked for small-size milks," the man complained.

"I'm sorry, sir, but this is the small size," Jessica said evenly, fighting an urge to pour both glasses of milk over his head. She intentionally mixed up the other glasses, placing the diet soda in front of the man and the unnaturally pink strawberry milk shake by his slim wife. *Why not?* she figured. This was one big tip she already knew she could write off. *Besides, the guy really is a fat pig. A diet soda would do him some good.* She ignored the man's glare as he pointedly switched the glasses.

Jessica turned wordlessly and began trudging back toward the kitchen.

"Oh, waitress!" a voice called from behind her. "Are you ever going to take our order?"

Jessica whirled angrily. Then she relaxed. The voice belonged to Winston Egbert, Sweet Valley High's official class clown. This summer he was also the head of beach maintenance at the marina. Winston was sitting at table two, in Jessica's section, and he was grinning broadly. Maria Santelli, Bruce Patman, and Amy Sutton were with him.

Jessica clenched her fist in a mock threat. "I swear, Winston, you don't know how close you just came to getting pushed through that picture window and right into the marina."

"Touchy, touchy, Wakefield," Bruce said smoothly. He glanced around the sunny restaurant. "You know, the service in this place used to be so friendly and efficient. But you just can't get good help nowadays. It seems like they'll hire pretty much anyone."

But Maria's brown eyes were full of sympathy. "How's it going?" she asked Jessica. "You look like you're having a rough day."

Jessica smiled. Maria was on the cheerleading squad with her at school and usually showed a lot of sense—despite the fact that she was dating a nerd like Winston. "To tell you the truth," Jessica said, "most of the day has been a lot of fun."

Winston raised his eyebrows. "If a fun day makes you want to throw me through a pane of glass, I'd hate to be here on a bad one."

Bruce flashed his handsome, smug grin. "Actually, Egbert, I often find myself wanting to push you through windows. It's a common response to your jokes."

"Tell us about your first day on the job," Amy urged, ignoring the boys' jibes.

"It's only the last hour or so that's made me feel like a punching bag," Jessica said. "Before that, it was really cool. You wouldn't believe the glamorous people I've met!"

Wealthy, well-connected Bruce leaned back and crossed his arms. "Actually, *I* probably would."

"Hadn't you heard, Jessica?" Winston asked.

"Bruce holds the patent on glamorous people around here. You're not allowed to meet any without scheduling it through his personal secretary."

"Egbert, why don't you save Wakefield and me the trouble and throw yourself through that window?"

Maria put a hand over each of the boys' mouths. "Shut up, you guys. Come on, Jess. Tell us about the people you've met."

"Well, I served one couple who just came up the coast from Mexico in a yacht as big as our whole high school—you know, slightly smaller than Bruce's bathtub." She stuck out her tongue at Bruce. "There was a man from Seattle who says he manages rock stars, but he was a crummy tipper. And I met a woman who sailed up in a strange-looking boat called a skipjack— I saw it out the window. She left me a thirty percent tip! Right after that, Lila stopped by at my break time, and we had lunch on the beach."

"Wow!" Bruce breathed. "You had lunch with *the* Lila Fowler? You said glamorous, but I thought you meant relatively unimportant people, like mere corporate moguls and world leaders. I had no idea—"

"Shut up, Bruce!" Bruce and Lila, the two richest students at Sweet Valley High, had been rivals for as long as Jessica could remember. But Jessica had more immediate concerns than whether Bruce or Lila was more deserving of the Most Rich and Snobby Award. She'd just spotted Mr. Jenkins peering out the door from the kitchen. "Be good, you guys. My boss is giving me dirty looks."

"You'd better take our order while we talk," Amy suggested, picking up her menu. "Who's first?"

"I'll have a sparkling mineral water and the avocado salad," Maria said. "Really, Jess, you look kind of frazzled. You've been at this all day. Can't you take five and sit down with us?"

Jessica did feel frazzled, at least in contrast to Amy. As usual Amy was dressed to the hilt, and not a strand of long blond hair was out of place.

Jessica shook her head. "I'd better not, although I admit my feet are killing me." She wrinkled her nose. "And that fat guy with the two bratty kids is probably the world's most obnoxious customer. I hate having to be nice to people who are jerks."

She glanced at Bruce as she said it—but not too conspicuously. Bruce could be a jerk, but he was a rich jerk. And she needed all the tips she could get.

"I'll have crab salad and an almond-flavored cappuccino," Winston said. "The crabmeat is from the *legs* of the crab, isn't it?"

Jessica raised her eyebrows. It wasn't the kind of order she had expected from Winston. "Of course it is," she assured him, though she had no idea what part of the crab it was from. She dutifully wrote his order on her pad.

"No, no, no," Winston said, shaking his head. "On second thought, I think I'll go with the salmon quiche. And mineral water. Sparkling mineral water, with lemon. But I'd like extra radishes on the salad. And instead of the ranch dressing, could you put blue cheese on it? No, let's make it half blue cheese and half Italian. You can do that, can't you?"

Jessica gritted her teeth. "Anything for you, Sir Egbert."

As soon as she rewrote the order, Winston spoke up again. "You know, Jessica, that pasta special on the blackboard sounded awfully good. Is that black pepper or white pepper on the fettuccine?"

Jessica crossed her arms and glowered at him, using her best Lila Fowler look of disdain.

Winston grinned. "OK, make it a double cheeseburger with everything on it, a big order of fries, and a chocolate milk shake."

"You might as well be at the Dairi Burger," Maria said.

"A man needs a hearty meal after a day of backbreaking work in the blazing sun."

Bruce laughed. "Come off it, Egbert. You're no more than the beach janitor."

"I prefer to think of myself as a coastal enhancement engineer."

"Oh, Elizabeth!" Mr. Jenkins's voice rang out from across the room.

"That's strange," Amy said. "I don't see Elizabeth anywhere."

Jessica shrugged. "A few minutes ago I saw her heading to the walk-in refrigerator in the back, for mayonnaise or something. But it's not my problem."

"Elizabeth!" the restaurant manager called again. Jessica realized too late that he was motioning toward her.

"Oops," she said to her friends. "I forgot. He

couldn't tell Liz and me apart if his life depended on it."

Mr. Jenkins stalked across the room and pulled her aside. "Elizabeth, the order for table five has been ready for some time. You're going to have to move a little faster."

Jessica shrugged. Table five was Mr. Obnoxious and the rest of his stupid family. "Sorry, Mr. Jenkins. I'll be finished taking this order in just a sec."

"Tut-tut," Winston said when the manager was out of earshot. "You must learn to be faster, Jessica. He's right, you know. I always prefer fast women myself."

Jessica gave him another Lila stare, wishing she could shoot arrows out of her eyes. Luckily Winston was basically a nice guy—it was one of the reasons she usually found him dull. At least he'd feel obligated to leave her a decent tip. It was more than she was expecting to get from the guy at table five—who was now tapping his watch and glaring at her.

Jessica sighed. One thing was obvious—she was infinitely better suited to giving orders than she was to taking them.

"After ten years in prison, there's not much I don't know about picking a lock," John Marin said under his breath. He slid a metal file into the crack alongside the back door of the house on Calico Drive. He smiled when he felt the lock give way. "Old Louie the Locksmith taught me well," he said, giving a silent thanks to the convict who'd had the cell next to his in the state penitentiary.

Inside, the Wakefields' dog was barking. Marin opened the door and stuck his head in. "Be quiet, you mongrel," he growled, baring his teeth. The golden retriever shrank back. "Some watchdog you are. Old Ned is awfully complacent. If he had any sense, the place would be guarded by pit bulls—" He sneered. "Not that they'd do any good against me."

Marin gazed at the Spanish-tiled kitchen, eyes narrow. "Well, Counselor. You've certainly done well for yourself since we last met," he said. "Soon it'll be time to pay the price." He grabbed a green apple from a bowl on the table, tossed it into the air, and caught it. Then he took a bite, grimaced, and left the apple on the table. "Sour."

He sauntered into the living room, with Prince Albert, the dog, following at a respectful distance. A collection of family photographs, each in a silver frame, was grouped on one shelf of the wall unit. Marin selected a framed Christmas card that showed the entire Wakefield family dressed as elves.

"Ah, Alice," he said, poking a finger at Ned Wakefield's pretty blond wife. "I could teach you all about Wonderland. Better watch yourself, dear. You wouldn't want to fall down any rabbit holes. And that Steven's a regular chip off the old block." He laughed. "Maybe later. For now, I'll stick with the twins—they bring out all those protective, paternalistic instincts that make Ned such a pathetically easy target."

Marin stuffed the photograph into his backpack and looked around the room once more.

It wouldn't do to get caught in the Wakefield house; it wasn't time yet. But Marin wasn't in a hurry—the family would be away for hours. "Information," he said to the dog. "I need more information."

Prince Albert trotted upstairs, and Marin followed. "I'm going to know everything there is to know about Jessica and Elizabeth Wakefield," he promised aloud. "And then I'll make my move. By the time I'm finished with those little girls, their daddy is going to wish he'd never gone to law school."

Chapter 4

Elizabeth balanced her tray on one arm as she jabbed at the button on the soft drink dispenser behind the counter. Ginger ale bubbled from the spigot.

"Jane!" she called as the more experienced waitress passed. "There's something wrong with the ginger ale! It's almost all foam."

"No problem, honey," Jane told her. "Each tap hooks up to two canisters—one for syrup and one for soda. See them here in back? The ginger ale syrup must be empty. I'll check it."

"I knew waitressing was hard work, but I had no idea there were so many things to learn!"

"You're doing swell for your first day, kid," Jane said. "Yep, that's it, all right. We need to replace the syrup canister. Watch and I'll show you how. There's nothing to it." She began unhooking the empty canister from the tube that connected it to the drink dispenser. "I might as well make myself useful. I don't dare set foot in the dining room until the kitchen gets me a bowl of clam chowder for table nine."

"Mr. Jenkins said you've worked here four summers in a row. Do you go to school the rest of the year?"

"Sweet Valley University, class of last week," Jane said proudly. "Pull over one of those fresh canisters, would you, Elizabeth? Make sure it says ginger ale."

"So you just graduated from college?" Elizabeth asked, surprised. She'd assumed Jane was at least in her mid-twenties.

Jane grinned. "I know, you're too polite to say it. But I don't look twenty-two. Actually, I'm an ancient twenty-six. I took a few years off after high school to work full time and save up some money."

She pressed the button on the drink dispenser and waited a few seconds until she was satisfied with the color of the ginger ale that poured out. "That looks about right," she said. "Try it now."

Elizabeth stuck the glass under the spigot and watched it fill up.

"At this rate I'll be a student until I'm old and gray," Jane said. "But I'm starting graduate school in the fall, so I figured I'd spend one last summer with Old Man Jenkins."

Elizabeth rolled her eyes. "He's kind of a strange little man, isn't he?"

Jane shrugged and wiped some syrup from the counter. "He's a boss. All bosses are strange."

"I just wish he'd get my name right for once. He's convinced that my sister Jessica is me, and that she's

41

perfect. But he thinks I'm a total screwup."

Jane laughed knowingly as she grabbed a basket of oyster crackers from a shelf under the counter. "He called me Jean for the entire first summer I was here. The second summer it was Joan. And last year I was Jan. I had to come back a fourth summer just to give him another chance to get it straight." She nudged the kitchen door open with her shoulder and called in to the head cook. "Samantha! I'm still waiting on that bowl of clam chowder for table nine!"

"What do you like most about working here?" Elizabeth fished her order pad out of her apron pocket and began double checking the orders for who she thought would be her last few customers of the day.

"Mostly I do it for the people," Jane confided. "This place gets the most interesting customers. I'm a sociology major, so I tell myself it's research."

"I know what you mean. For some reason people who own boats almost always turn out to be fascinating."

Jane nodded. "Speaking of fascinating, look at that fine specimen who just walked in. I swear, if I were ten years younger—"

Elizabeth laughed when she saw the new customer. It was Todd. "Don't say another word. He's taken."

"Story of my life, Liz. All the good ones are. Samantha! I'm still waiting on that chowder!"

A few minutes later Elizabeth had served her

final customer. She waved good-bye to Jane and to Jessica, then greeted Todd with a smile.

"How was your first day?" he asked as he held open the door for her.

"Great!" She gave him a quick kiss. "But my feet are ready to go on strike. I think I'm getting blisters on my blisters. How are the windsurfing lessons?"

"I still can't believe people are paying me to play in the water all day!"

"Any ideas for dinner tonight after the movie?" Elizabeth asked as they walked toward Todd's black BMW.

"How about the Dairi Burger?"

Elizabeth shrugged. "If we're going to be in a rut, we might as well be consistent about it."

Todd stared at her. "What's that supposed to mean?"

"Nothing. The Dairi Burger is fine."

She climbed into the BMW and sank back gratefully into the leather upholstery. She concentrated on the colorful boats of the marina and the jazz music that Todd had slipped into the tape deck.

"Now *that* was a hot car!" he exclaimed suddenly as they pulled out of the parking lot.

"Where?" Elizabeth wrenched her gaze away from the boats, but all she caught was a flash of red that blurred by them as it sped back toward the café.

Todd glanced in the rearview mirror. "A brand-new Miata convertible, fire-engine red. The guy driving looked only a few years older than us."

"If he's going into the Marina Café, someone

ought to warn him to stay away from Jessica's section!"

"Uh-oh! Beware the wrath of the evil twin. What's Jessica's latest crisis?"

"She's dying to go home, but one customer is lingering forever over coffee. Jess won't leave without that tip. But she's totally ticked off."

Todd laughed. "In other words, anyone who asks Jessica for anything right now may just find himself staring down the sharp end of a butter knife."

"Can I, uh, get you anything else?" Jessica asked, staring expectantly at the college-age woman at table four. She gestured at the untouched bill on the table. "I can get your change for you anytime you're ready."

The woman looked up from her book. "Oh, just another coffee refill, please."

Jessica sighed and stalked back across the room to the coffeepot behind the counter. "I can't believe this!" she screeched at Jane. "She's had about sixty cups of coffee!"

Jane laughed. "Some people just like to hang out here—the scenery's good." She gestured toward the walls of windows that surrounded three sides of the dining room. Boats bobbed at the docks, their sails colored orange by the day's last hour of sunlight. Through the window Jessica could see the flash of Elizabeth's turquoise shirt as she kissed Todd and climbed into his BMW.

"Some people get to go home at a reasonable hour," Jessica complained.

Watching the warmth between Todd and Elizabeth, Jessica was surprised at how much she missed Ken. When it came to dating, she'd always said she liked being a free agent. But it would be nice to know she had someone waiting to take her out at the end of her shift.

"Cheer up," Jane urged. "You're probably scoring brownie points with Mr. Jenkins for staying late. I bet he's in the back room right now, thinking about how dedicated you are."

"Right," Jessica scoffed. "Only he probably thinks I'm Elizabeth."

"You should be counting your blessings," Jane said, pointing at the coffee-drinking college student. "Customers who read at the table are pretty undemanding. At least she's not a pain in the neck."

"What do you mean, she's not a pain in the neck? She won't leave! How long can she sit there reading?"

"Are you kidding? I caught sight of that textbook she's wading through. It's for a sociology course I took a few years back—Human Systems and Structures 101. Each chapter takes about two pots of coffee to get through."

"But I wanted to catch this last hour of sun! How am I going to keep my tan if I never get out of here until the middle of the night?"

"Why don't you go on home, kid? I'll take care of her coffee refills, and I'll save the tip for you. If you're lucky, I might not even take a cut."

Jessica hesitated. She felt a twinge of guilt at the thought of letting Jane take over for her.

"Of course," Jane continued, "college students are always broke, so they're lousy tippers."

"Well, I'm glad to know it'll be worth the wait," Jessica said glumly. Suddenly she caught sight of a shiny red convertible pulling into the parking lot. It was the kind of car that a big tipper drove. "Thanks for offering," she said quickly. "But I think I'll stick around. As long as I'm trapped here, maybe somebody else will come in. Somebody who tips really well."

Jane nodded. "Then would you mind giving me a yell if table ten seems low on anything? I've got some work to do in the storage room."

Jessica stepped closer to the window that overlooked the parking lot. "And I've got some work to do here," she said under her breath. With the sun in her eyes she didn't have a good view of the driver, but she knew that the car was a new Miata.

She willed the car's owner to walk into the café rather than out along the docks. *"Yes!"* she said aloud when he turned up the walkway.

The college student looked up from her reading. Jessica smiled an apology and set up a table for her new customer.

"Can I help you?" she asked. "I've got a lovely table, right over . . ." Jessica's voice trailed off as she looked for the first time at the driver's face. He was drop-dead gorgeous. About twenty years old, he was tall, with wavy brown hair and deep blue eyes.

"I sure hope you can," he said easily, flashing her a dazzling smile. "Just a table for one, nonsmoking."

"Um, uh, sure," Jessica stammered. "As you can see, there are plenty of tables open. Would you like to be near a window?"

"Whatever you think," he said with another grin. "I'll place myself in your hands."

Sounds good to me. The man's chiseled features had caught her attention first; now she was beginning to notice the rest of him. His purple brushed-silk shirt accentuated his broad shoulders, which practically cried out for her fingers to touch them. *Yes,* she decided. *"In my hands" would be a very fine place for him.*

"You did say a table for *one,* didn't you?" Jessica asked as she led him to her best table. "I mean, you're not meeting someone here?"

"Nope," he said. "I just got to town, and I don't know a soul. So it's just me."

Jessica smiled back. "Can I get you anything to start? A drink?"

"Mineral water, please. And maybe a little bit of information, if you don't mind."

Jessica was intrigued. Maybe this was a classy way of asking for her phone number. She slowly tucked a stray lock of hair behind her ear and gave him a flirtatious smile. "What kind of information?"

"Do you know the area well?"

Jessica shrugged. "Sure. I've lived here all my life."

The man grinned again. He had the whitest teeth Jessica had ever seen. "That's perfect," he said. "I was hoping to meet somebody just like you."

Jessica smiled. Customer service had never been so easy. "Well, you found me. What can I do for you?"

"I'm sorry. I should have started from the beginning. My name's Scott Maderlake," he said, extending a hand. When Jessica shook it, she felt a tingle like an electric current run through her body.

"I'm Jessica Wakefield. What are you in town for—business or pleasure?"

He raised his eyebrows. "I'm here on business, but I'm beginning to think this could be a pleasurable place to be." He paused. "I work for Jillian DeRiggi. You've heard of her, of course?"

"Oh, of course," Jessica lied, racking her brain to figure out who Jillian DeRiggi might be. It certainly sounded like an important name.

"Jillian is producing a new television miniseries," he explained. "It's about a southern California high school. I'm traveling up the coast, scouting possible locations."

Jessica's eyes widened. Not only was Scott gorgeous, but he might be able to get her a part in a television miniseries. She silently thanked the bookish, coffee-drinking college student for keeping her late at work.

"So you'll go back to Jillian DeRiggi and tell her where to film her miniseries?" Jessica asked. "I guess that means you would decide what local landmarks and, um, *people* should be in it."

Scott laughed. "Decide is too strong a word," he said. "Really I'm only an intern."

"But I'll bet you have a lot of influence."

"With Jillian? She does seem to trust me. But the real reason they send people like me on these advance trips is that it would cost a fortune to have someone important do the initial location scouting. After I narrow it down to a few places that meet the criteria, Jillian will visit those sites herself and make a final decision."

"She should definitely use Sweet Valley," Jessica said. "It's perfect for your miniseries. I'm sure of it."

"So far, I like the scenery just fine," Scott said.

Jessica was almost sure he was flirting with her. "Maybe I could show you more of it," she suggested.

Scott looked straight into her eyes. "That's the best offer I've had all day. Can you start by answering a few questions?"

"Sure! Ask away." She pulled out her order pad. "But if you're planning to order something, maybe you should do it now. My boss is in the back, but he could look out here anytime. He might as well think I'm hard at work."

"Your secret is safe with me," Scott said, opening his menu. "I'll have the crab salad. And the answer to the following question: When they're not serving salads, what do the really popular, attractive teenagers do around here for fun?"

Jessica smiled warmly. He was positively flirting with her. "Mostly we show television interns around town. When that gets tedious, we bring them to a place called the Dairi Burger, which is where everyone important hangs out."

"And where do they go when they want to be alone?"

Jessica pretended to consider the question thoughtfully, but her heart was racing. "Oh, I can think of a few places," she said slowly. "Secca Lake and Miller's Point come to mind."

"Secca Lake I've heard of."

Jessica nodded. "I'm not surprised. It's beautiful. I bet it would look great on film. And Miller's Point is even better—for a lot of reasons." She thought of all the nights she'd parked at Miller's Point with one boyfriend or another, kissing and gazing at the twinkling lights of the valley below. She would love to show Miller's Point to Scott Maderlake—but as more than just research for a television miniseries.

"There are also a lot of places in town for a romantic dinner," she added hopefully.

"What about the high school?"

"I suppose that's OK for a romantic dinner—if you're into mystery meat and fluorescent lighting," Jessica joked.

Scott laughed. "Forget dinner. As I said, Jillian's new miniseries is set at a high school. Tell me about Sweet Valley High."

"I've got a better idea," Jessica responded. "Why don't I take you there?"

"I thought you'd never ask. Are you free tomorrow afternoon?"

Jessica looked into his midnight-blue eyes and felt a delicious tingle run down her spine. "I can arrange to be."

Ned Wakefield sauntered into the empty house Monday evening and tossed a stack of mail onto the kitchen table. Prince Albert padded in from the living room; Mr. Wakefield stroked the golden retriever's furry head.

"Hey, boy," he said. "What were you doing in the living room? I thought I shut that door before I left this morning. I guess I was really on edge. I must've forgotten."

He pulled out a chair. The gentle scraping of wood against the Spanish-tile floor sounded loud in the empty house. Someone had left a green apple sitting on the table, with one ragged brown circle where a bite had been taken. Somebody in the house obviously needed a lecture on not leaving out food—most likely, the culprit was Steven.

Mr. Wakefield seemed to have the house to himself. He and Steven had left the law office at the same time, but Steven had driven to the mall to pick up a few things for his trip to Sacramento in the morning. And Mrs. Wakefield wouldn't be home for another hour; she had a late meeting with the fireplace-in-the-bathroom client. As for the girls . . .

Mr. Wakefield bit his lip, thinking of Jessica and Elizabeth. It was still early. They'd probably be breezing through the door at any minute, full of stories about their first day on the job.

He grabbed a soda from the refrigerator and sat at the table. "What's in today's mail, Albert?" The dog's expression looked so alert and intelligent that

Mr. Wakefield half expected him to answer. Instead he answered himself as he sifted through the stack. "Telephone bill, electricity bill, junk mail, junk mail, junk mail, letter from Steven's girlfriend . . . And what's this one?"

He held up a plain, blood-red envelope. It looked like the kind of envelope that Christmas cards came in, but nobody would send a Christmas card in June. He turned it over in his hand. No return address. It didn't even have a postmark—obviously someone had slipped it into the mailbox. He shrugged and slit open the envelope. Then he frowned. "Now why would someone send us our own Christmas card from last year?"

Mr. Wakefield remembered the photograph well. Jessica had talked the rest of the family into posing in red-and-green elf costumes. Even Prince Albert peered out from under a floppy Santa hat.

But this copy of the photograph had been ruined. Across the family's faces someone had scrawled a message in heavy black ink, using large, angular letters:

Nice family, Ned. I especially like the girls. JM

Mr. Wakefield felt the color drain from his face. Where had Marin scrounged up one of the Wakefield family's old Christmas cards? They'd sent them all to family friends—except for the print that was framed in the living room.

Suddenly Mr. Wakefield thought of Prince Albert walking in from the living room. He stared at the green apple with one bite missing.

He shook his head. "No. It's impossible," he whispered. "He couldn't have been in the house."

In a daze, Mr. Wakefield rose from his chair and walked into the living room. By the time he reached the collection of family pictures arranged on one shelf of the wall unit, Ned knew exactly what he would find—a conspicuously empty spot where the Christmas photograph had been. Moments later, his heart stopped. John Marin hadn't forgotten—not by a long shot.

Chapter 5

"What do you mean, you can't prevent him from coming after my family?" Mr. Wakefield shouted into the phone. "What good is the police department if—"

"Ned, you're an attorney," said his friend Tony Cabrini, a police detective. "You know the law. We can't seek out this guy and haul him into jail just because of a threat he made ten years ago. That doesn't constitute probable cause, and you know it."

"I've got more than a ten-year-old threat. I received another one this evening. I'm telling you, Tony, this guy is a maniac! And he was in my house today!"

"Can you prove that?"

"Sorry. He forgot to leave his signed confession."

"There's no law against sending Christmas cards. And complimenting you on your children hardly constitutes a threat—"

Mr. Wakefield felt his face turning red. "It sure as

hell does! Dammit, Tony, I know what he meant—"

"Calm down, Ned. I agree that this guy is danger-ous. But *legally* 'nice family, Ned,' is not a menacing remark. I shouldn't have to tell you that. You know as well as I do that the public defender's office would have a field day if we arrested Marin without any more evidence than that."

"So what can I do about him?"

"A guy who would leave a note like that obviously enjoys making you sweat. My bet is that you'll be re-ceiving more of them. As soon as we can establish a pattern of threatening statements, we can pick the guy up."

"You're telling me that all I can do is sit around and check my mail?"

"For now, yes," the detective admitted. "In the meantime, we'll try to locate Marin so we can keep tabs on him. I'll talk with his parole officer tonight and call you back in the morning. If this guy violates parole even once, then we can move in on him."

"And what if that's too late?"

"I'm sorry, Ned, but it's the best I can do for now. Until we can prove that Marin has done something that's against the law, we don't have a case."

Elizabeth sighed as she walked out of the movie theater with Todd that night. "What a great movie!" she breathed.

Todd took her hand. "Sure, *Roman Holiday* is a good one. But what is this—the third time you've seen it?"

"Fourth, actually. But I never identified with Audrey Hepburn the way I did this time. I can really understand how much she needed to get out and do something different."

Todd snorted. "It's rough being a princess, with everything you could ever want handed to you on a silver platter."

"Everything except adventure! And freedom!" Elizabeth cried. "The only way she could get them was to break out of her boring, oppressive life—even if it did mean shocking everybody."

Todd looked at her strangely. "You're sounding pretty intense tonight, Liz. Are you OK?"

Elizabeth smiled weakly. "Oh, I'm fine. I just envy her for having the courage to break free and find a real adventure."

"And you envy her for finding Gregory Peck."

"That too. Especially since he was playing a writer. Jealous?"

"Insanely. And hungry. Come on, let's hit the Dairi Burger."

When Jessica strolled through the door that night, her father's voice was like a thunderclap. *"Young lady, where in the world have you been?"*

He was pacing in the living room while Mrs. Wakefield sat on the couch, her hands folded.

"I asked you a question!"

Jessica stared at him. "I was at Lila's. Remember, I called and said I wouldn't be home for dinner."

"Dinner was hours ago! It's almost ten o'clock!"

"So? You knew where I was. What's the problem?"

"The problem is that your mother and I were worried. When you said you wouldn't be home for dinner, I assumed that meant you'd be home soon after dinner. You didn't say anything about staying out so late."

"I'm sixteen years old, Dad. You have no right to treat me like a baby!"

"I'm your father. And if you can't take a little responsibility for your actions, then you don't deserve to be treated like an adult. How did we know you weren't lying in a ditch somewhere—"

His voice broke off, and he sat down weakly. Jessica just gaped at him. She'd seen her father angry before, but seldom this unreasonable.

"Ned, she *did* call to let us know where she was," Mrs. Wakefield reminded him gently.

"I know," he said, staring at his hands. "You're both right. I'm overreacting. But Jessica, there have been some crimes in the neighborhood lately. It's gotten me a little anxious, especially about you and your sister."

"Crimes?" Jessica asked. "I haven't heard of any crimes. What happened?"

"There's no need to worry about anything," Mr. Wakefield said quickly.

"Honey, I hadn't heard about any local crimes either," Mrs. Wakefield said. "Was anybody hurt?"

"No, no. Of course not. I guess it hasn't been on the news. I just heard about it around the courthouse today." He jumped up suddenly. "What time is Elizabeth coming home?"

"Ned, she said she'd be here by eleven. Don't worry about her. She's with Todd. You know how responsible they both are."

Jessica gritted her teeth. People were always raving about how responsible her twin was.

"Yes, of course," Ned said. "If Elizabeth and Todd say they'll be here by eleven, then they'll be here by eleven." He scrutinized his watch. "I think I'll go upstairs to see if Steven needs help packing for his trip." He stalked out of the room, but Jessica noticed that he turned into his den instead of going up the stairs.

"What's eating him?" Jessica asked, annoyed. "It's bad enough getting in trouble all the time for doing something wrong. But I didn't break a rule or miss a curfew or anything this time. It's not fair!"

Mrs. Wakefield smiled. "Sorry, sweetheart. But your father's been tense all day. I'm sure he'll be himself after a good night's sleep."

"I hope so. He's been acting possessed since this morning."

"You're looking a little worn out yourself, Jess. I know what hard work waitressing can be. Why don't you go on and get to bed early?"

Jessica yawned. "You're right. I am tired. Good night."

A minute later Jessica skipped up the stairs, silently thanking her father for making everyone forget that she was supposed to have vacuumed the living room.

Prince Albert wagged his tail and watched as Mr. Wakefield sat down at his desk. Mr. Wakefield struggled to catch his breath. He had to control his nerves better. He didn't want to terrify the rest of the family by telling them about Marin. But if he kept acting paranoid, they would quickly figure out that something was seriously wrong.

On the other hand, he thought, *if I warned them of the danger, maybe the twins would take extra precautions. Maybe they'd be able to protect themselves.*

"No," he said aloud to the dog. "There's no way they can protect themselves against a maniac like Marin. And what kind of precautions would help? I can't lock them in their bedrooms, under guard, until Marin forgets about them."

As soon as his hands were steady Mr. Wakefield dialed the telephone.

"Tony, I'm sorry to call you at home this late, but I couldn't wait until morning. Have you found out anything else?"

Detective Cabrini's voice was full of regret. "Nothing you're going to like. The address Marin gave his parole officer was a fake. We don't know where to find him."

Mr. Wakefield felt as if he'd been pushed off a cliff. He clutched the receiver as if it were a lifeline. "So what's next?"

"The phony address constitutes a parole violation. That means we can pick him up if we find him. Unfortunately we have no idea where he is."

"How can we locate the scumbag?"

"*You* sit home and let the police take care of it. I put out an APB an hour ago. First thing in the morning, I'll have people start tracking down any known associates of Marin's. Don't worry, Ned. We'll get this guy."

"Thanks, Tony," Mr. Wakefield said in a controlled voice. "Keep me informed."

Slowly he placed the receiver in its cradle. A moment later he realized he was still gripping it. He unwrapped his fingers from the receiver and pulled out his address book. "If the police can't keep my daughters safe from John Marin, then I'll call someone who can," he said aloud. He found the entry he was looking for and dialed the home number of James Battaglia, a private investigator he knew from a case they'd worked on together the year before.

"Jim? This is Ned Wakefield. Sorry to call so late, but I have a dangerous situation on my hands."

In Todd's car on the way to the Dairi Burger, Elizabeth couldn't stop thinking about *Roman Holiday*.

"You know," she said thoughtfully, twirling a golden curl around her finger, "I'm feeling a little like that princess, trapped in a boring routine."

"How can you be trapped in a boring routine?" Todd asked. "School just ended Friday. And today was your first day in a new job."

"Well, yes," Elizabeth said. "But that's not exactly what I meant. It's kind of hard to explain. It's bigger than that. Basically, I feel as if it doesn't matter whether school is in session or not. My life stays pretty much the same. I see the same people, day in and day out." She gestured toward the lighted sign of the Dairi Burger just ahead. "I go to the same places."

"We could go to Guido's Pizza tonight, if you'd rather," Todd offered.

Elizabeth shook her head. "No, that wouldn't make any difference! I've been to every place within ten miles of here, over and over again, for my whole life."

Todd shrugged and steered the BMW into the crowded parking lot of the Dairi Burger.

And he even pulls into the same parking space he always uses, Elizabeth thought with a sigh. "Don't you ever wish that something different would happen?"

"Why? I like things the way they are." Suddenly Todd's eyes opened wider. "Elizabeth, are you trying to tell me something about our relationship? You don't want to date other people, do you?"

"Oh, no, Todd! It's nothing like that!"

"Then what brought all this on?" he asked as they walked toward the restaurant. "I just don't get it. You're talking as if seeing that movie was a life-changing experience. It was just a romantic comedy!"

Inside the restaurant Elizabeth breathed the familiar Dairi Burger aroma of french fries and hamburgers. "Have you ever wondered what it would be like to walk into this place and smell something totally different, like Indian curries or a Thai stir-fry?"

"Were we watching the same movie?"

Elizabeth laughed. "Sorry, I guess I'm sounding kind of weird."

"Look, there's a booth about to open up!" Todd said, negotiating his way through the crowded dining room. "Let's grab it."

They settled into a booth at one end of the noisy room, waving at a few friends they spotted at nearby tables. *"I see the same people, day in and day out,"* Elizabeth repeated under her breath. She wished Gregory Peck would materialize at the next booth.

"What can I get you to drink?" asked a young, gum-chewing waitress a few minutes later.

"Two root beers," Todd said.

"No!" Elizabeth interrupted, more loudly than she'd intended. "I mean, I'm in the mood for something different." She turned to the waitress. "You don't have iced cappuccino, do you?"

The waitress blew a bubble. "Nope."

"How about iced coffee, then?"

The waitress shrugged. "Sure, why not? We got coffee. We got ice cubes."

"Do you want one too, Todd?" Elizabeth asked hopefully.

"No, I'll stick with my plain old root beer." He looked up at the impatient waitress. "I'm trapped in a boring routine," he explained.

Elizabeth watched her boyfriend's strong, handsome features and knew that he didn't have the slightest idea what was bothering her. She loved

Todd, but sometimes he was so . . . *down-to-earth.* Normally she liked that about him. But right now, it was annoying. Why couldn't Todd be a little more of a dreamer? Why did he have to be so eternally *contented*? If nothing else, she wished that she could at least get him to understand what she was feeling.

"Your root beer and your iced coffee will be coming right up," the waitress told them. She turned away from the table.

"Oh, can you make my coffee with half-and-half?" Elizabeth asked.

"All right," the waitress said in the same clipped voice that Elizabeth had heard herself use with an irritating customer a few hours earlier. "That's one boring, routine root beer and one iced coffee with half-and-half."

"And three sugars."

The waitress shrugged. "And three sugars," she repeated slowly as she wrote it on her order pad.

"Oh, and I'd like a straw."

"Naturally."

Once they were alone, Todd took her hand in both of his. "So how are you, Liz, really?" he asked. "I can't believe that seeing *Roman Holiday* could make you unhappy with your whole life."

Elizabeth shook her head. "I didn't say that I'm unhappy with my life. I love my life, Todd. I love you!" She said it vehemently, but deep down, Elizabeth wondered if she had experienced enough of life to know what real love felt like. Todd was fun, but he wasn't necessarily . . . *a soul mate.* Of course, she couldn't tell him that.

"I just want an adventure," she concluded lamely. "Something different."

"Like Audrey Hepburn, escaping the palace."

"Exactly! But it's not just the movie. There was something Jessica said to me this morning—"

Todd rolled his eyes. "Oh, I get it now. It figures that your psycho sister would have something to do with this."

"She's not a psycho, and you know it! Besides, what she said made a lot of sense."

"Jessica made sense? And you said nothing unusual ever happens."

"Cut it out. All Jessica did was point out the fact that I'm in a rut, and that I'll never be a great writer if I haven't experienced anything interesting to write about."

Todd snapped his fingers. "I've got it! I'll help you overthrow the government! Then you can write one of those techno-espionage thrillers while we spend the rest of our lives in prison. Or we can rent ourselves out as assassins so you can write murder mysteries. Or I'll buy you a horse, and you can write westerns."

"That's not exactly what I had in mind."

"What then?"

"Working at the café today really opened my eyes. You wouldn't believe the fascinating people who come into a place like that. Todd, there's a whole world out there!"

"But you knew that before."

"Yes, I did. But today I talked to a woman who's just back from three months in Hawaii, studying volcanoes. One family was sailing out to Catalina to spend the whole summer camping and hiking. And another customer was on a cruise from Baja all the way up the coast to Alaska, just to see what's there!"

"You want to sail to Alaska?"

"I want to experience *life*!"

"I thought this *was* life. And you've always raved about how much you love Sweet Valley. Now you're telling me that one day of meeting yacht owners has changed all that?"

"It's not just the one day of meeting yacht owners."

"Oh, I forgot about Audrey Hepburn and Jessica. In that case, it makes perfect sense."

"Don't be sarcastic, Todd. I'm serious about this."

"I can tell you are. But Liz, I really don't get it."

Elizabeth jumped at a snapping sound just over her head. The gum-popping waitress was back. "You two ready to order?"

"I'll have a bowl of clam chowder," Elizabeth said, pointing a finger at the most exotic thing on the menu.

The waitress popped her gum again. "I suppose you want that made with half-and-half."

"No, just the regular way."

The woman pulled a pencil out from behind her ear. "OK, that's one clam chowder, made the boring, routine way. And how about you, Mr. Adventure?"

Todd began to describe what he wanted on his Dairi Burger. Elizabeth could have recited it with him—cheese, ketchup, lettuce, tomato, and mustard, with no pickles or mayo, just like always.

After the waitress left, Todd changed the subject and began telling her about his windsurfing students. Elizabeth tried to listen, but she found herself focusing on Todd's neat, conservative haircut, his wholesome good looks, and his mall-store rugby shirt. He was so ordinary.

Of course, she'd hated it when Todd cut his hair in an urban-commando look and tried to grow a mustache. But that was just it. Even when Todd played at taking a walk on the wild side, he couldn't pull it off. It was just a game, and it didn't suit him. For the first time Elizabeth realized just how unsophisticated her boyfriend really was.

She sipped her iced coffee, trying to feel exciting, cultured, and cosmopolitan—like her customer who was sailing up the coast from Baja. But it was hard to feel exciting, cultured, and cosmopolitan in a room that was full of the same wholesome, small-town, teenage faces she'd seen every day for the last several years.

Her good friend Olivia Davidson gazed into Harry Minton's eyes, holding his hand. Just behind Elizabeth sat Amy Sutton and Caroline Pearce; she could hear enough bits and pieces of the conversation to know they were gossiping about guys, as always. Across the room, Rose Jameson appeared to be telling a funny story to Andrea Slade and Sally Larson. Bruce

Patman and Kirk Anderson sprawled on vinyl-covered stools at the counter, bragging loudly to each other about their victory in the season's final tennis match against Big Mesa High School.

In fact, except for Jessica—who was probably off with Lila somewhere—the place was full of the same people as always, having the same kinds of conversations they always had while eating their usual Dairi Burger orders.

Elizabeth wanted to scream.

Then her eyes fell on someone she hadn't noticed earlier. In the back corner of the restaurant a young man sat alone in a booth. He was scribbling furiously in a small, spiral-bound notebook. Elizabeth was intrigued.

He looked about twenty. A terrific tan set off his handsome features and showed above the neckline of a white T-shirt he wore with a navy windbreaker. His brown, wavy hair was a little lighter than Todd's. And it was disheveled, as if he'd been standing in the wind.

Suddenly he looked up, and their eyes locked. Elizabeth felt a jolt run through her body, like electricity. As his gaze met hers, it seemed to Elizabeth that time froze. Then he bent his head back down to his notebook and resumed his writing. But in those few seconds of eye contact, Elizabeth knew she had found the indefinable something she had been searching for. She had found her Gregory Peck.

She might have even found her soul mate.

Chapter 6

It was very early Tuesday morning, but John Marin was wide awake. Ideas raced through his mind in an intricate dance of vengeance and carefully laid plans. Finally he gave up on trying to sleep. He jumped out of bed, reached for his mini-recorder, and played back the tape of Ned Wakefield's conversation with the private investigator the evening before.

"I have a dangerous situation on my hands," Wakefield had begun, sounding terribly serious.

Marin laughed. "Much more dangerous than you imagine, Counselor," he said, sneering at the cassette tape as if it were Ned Wakefield himself. "For instance, you have no idea that I left a little present in your telephone receiver yesterday. You may not know it, Ned, but I made straight A's in the prison's wiretapping course. Of course the class was, shall we say, *extracurricular*."

68

He listened while Mr. Wakefield gave the private investigator the details of the case.

"You say his name is John Marin?" Battaglia asked, his voice crackling through the tape recorder as he spelled out the name.

"That's right," Wakefield answered. "What can you do?"

"If the police will cooperate, I'll coordinate with them as I begin trying to locate the guy. In the meantime, if Marin really is after your daughters, the best way to find him will be to stick close to the twins. I'll hire a man to watch them during the day while they're working at the restaurant."

"Battaglia's spy won't be the only one watching the little darlings," Marin said with a chuckle. He had already hired his own guy to keep an eye on Jessica and Elizabeth. The man was a little slow on the uptake, but very dependable—in other words, perfect for Marin's purposes.

"Good," Wakefield told the investigator. "And I'll ask Detective Cabrini to allow you access to the police files. In fact, I'll call him back right now and have him courier you over a photograph of Marin sometime tomorrow."

Marin stopped the tape machine. "Bingo!" That was exactly the bit he had wanted to hear again. Now all he had to do was replay the next conversation between Wakefield and Cabrini, and he'd know the details of the delivery of that photograph.

"Sorry, Counselor," Marin said with a smile. "But I wouldn't be surprised if a funny thing happens to

69

that mug shot on its way to Battaglia. I have a funny feeling your private investigator is going to end up with a photograph of the wrong man."

Elizabeth was only half listening to Jessica's chatter as the twins walked from the parking lot to the café Tuesday morning.

"Lila was going on and on last night about her new bathing suit," Jessica said. "Frankly, I think yellow is unflattering on brunettes. Why spend all that time perfecting your suntan if you're going to wear a color that makes you look all washed out?"

Elizabeth didn't care if Lila's tan looked washed out. She was too busy thinking about the mysterious guy she'd seen at the Dairi Burger the night before. She'd felt drawn to him, like steel to a magnet. But she wasn't sure why. He wasn't any more handsome than Todd. And she knew nothing at all about him; he could be a real creep. Elizabeth dismissed that thought immediately. It couldn't be true. Even from across the room, she'd seen her own longing for adventure and romance mirrored in his eyes.

Elizabeth realized she had stopped walking and was standing perfectly still at the base of the pier. Jessica, a few steps ahead, turned back and tapped the side of Elizabeth's head with her knuckles. "Earth to Liz! Earth to Liz! You haven't been listening to me!"

Elizabeth smiled sheepishly. "Sorry, Jess. I guess I was busy, uh, looking at the boats." She hadn't been. But as soon as Elizabeth said it, she found her imagination caught by the streamlined white hulls, as lovely as sculptures in the morning sunlight, with their billowy sails and scarlet and blue flags that fluttered in the breeze. She wished she could be on one of the gleaming decks, with nothing but sparkling blue ocean for miles around.

Jessica shook her head. "I think you've caught Dad's spacing-out disease. I didn't realize he was contagious."

"Aren't they beautiful?" Elizabeth said, gazing at the sailboats.

Jessica shrugged. "Sure. But I've got to get inside. Remember, Mr. Jenkins said I could leave after the lunch rush if I was here in time to help set up for breakfast. Are you coming in?"

"I'll be right there," Elizabeth said. For a moment she wondered why Jessica wanted to leave work early—she'd been so adamant about winning the tip contest. *She probably has a real emergency to take care of, like buying a new bathing suit to keep up with Lila's wardrobe.*

Elizabeth stood for a minute more, watching the gently bobbing boats. She imagined herself sailing to distant ports, where tile-roofed houses lined lush hillsides and the air was filled with the fragrance of wildflowers.

Suddenly the daydream vanished. Ten yards away, a man was fishing off the dock. He wore old, patched clothes, and half of his face was hidden under a big, floppy hat. Even at that distance Elizabeth could tell that the man needed a shave. A prickly feeling ran up

71

her spine. She couldn't see his eyes, but she was sure the man was watching her.

She hurried toward the restaurant, but she could still feel the stranger's eyes boring into her back.

An hour later Elizabeth set a tray of muffins on the counter of the Marina Café as Jessica reached for the coffeepot.

"Can you believe that guy at table five?" Jessica asked.

"The one who's dressed like he just stepped out of a bad novel about yachting?"

"That's the one. But get this—he says he started in Portugal and he's sailing around the world all by himself!"

"Sailing around the world?" Elizabeth's eyes seemed to lose focus. Her face took on a dreamy look, and Jessica stared at her curiously for a moment.

"He's stopped here for a few days to take a break from all that sailing," Jessica said. "But he's not like any sailor I've ever met."

"Right. And you've met so many. What's so different about this guy?"

"He ordered a peanut-butter-and-jelly sandwich and a Diet Coke!"

"First thing in the morning? That is kind of weird."

"I tried to tell him we don't have peanut butter and jelly on the menu. But then I figured, what the heck. So I'm making it for him myself and charging him the same price as an egg salad."

"Mr. Jenkins would be proud of you, Jessica."

Jessica laughed. "You mean Elizabeth."

"You're right," Elizabeth agreed. "He would say Elizabeth. Are you finished with that coffeepot? My customer said she'd fall asleep right at the table if I didn't get her some more caffeine, fast."

"Why don't you just give it to her intravenously?" Jessica asked, handing her the pot.

"Actually, that's how she asked for it," Elizabeth said over her shoulder. "But I'm not quite that dedicated to the theory that the customer is always right!"

"Ugh!" Jane complained, coming up behind Jessica. "Look at that guy walking in right now. What a loser!"

"Oh, great," Jessica said. "He's sitting down at my table. Hey, do you know where those little containers of half-and-half are?"

Jane pointed to a carton on a shelf behind the counter. "He sure doesn't look like he can afford much of a tip," she commented wryly.

Jessica stood on tiptoes to reach the box. "He doesn't look like he could afford a glass of water. What scruffy-looking clothes! He'll probably scare all the rich, generous customers away from my section."

"Here, let me reach that for you. I'm a couple inches taller." Jane handed her the box. Then she glanced back into the dining room and grinned. "You lucky devil! I think that creep likes you."

"Come off it, Jane."

"I'm serious. It's hard to see under that enormous hat he's wearing, but I'm almost positive that he's staring straight at you, no doubt with hunger in his eyes."

"Right, because he wants me to come and take his breakfast order. What do you wanna bet he orders a glass of water and maybe some of those little packages of oyster crackers?"

"And ketchup," Jane said with a laugh. "That'll definitely win the tip contest for you."

Jessica frowned. "I'm lousy at math, but it doesn't take a genius to know that fifteen percent of nothing is nothing."

"Cheer up. Maybe he's a filthy-rich codger who slinks around in rags because he wants to see who'll treat a poor man right. There could be an inheritance in it for you."

"I won't hold my breath—except maybe when I'm taking his order. He looks like he takes a bath about once every leap year." She grabbed a tray of muffins and coffee and hurried back to the dining room.

Jessica stood as far away from the haggard man as possible while she took his order for eggs and coffee. As she turned away from his table she caught sight of Lila sauntering in, her new yellow one-piece visible under a lacy white cover-up. Jessica was relieved to see her best friend; she could use some pleasant conversation. Besides, Lila could afford to tip well. Business in Jessica's section would be slow until that weird guy left.

"Hey, Lila!" Jessica called. "Sit over here. It's my section."

Lila eyed the man in the tattered hat. "Uh, I don't

74

know, Jess. The view is better over there." She pointed to the far side of the café.

"Lila Fowler, don't you dare!" Jessica glanced at the stranger again and sighed. She could see Lila's point. But what were friends for? She directed her to the table in her section that was farthest from her unkempt customer. "How's this?"

"I guess it'll do," Lila said uncertainly. "I still don't understand why you want to wait on people all summer. I mean, it's so tacky. It's like being a *servant.*"

Jessica shrugged. "We can't all be born millionaires—present company excepted, of course. Besides, it's not that bad. I've been meeting the most exciting, glamorous people here!"

Lila raised her eyebrows. "Oh, really? Like who? Mr. Clean over there, in the hat that's ten years out of style?"

"Forget about him," Jessica said. She pointed instead to the peanut-butter lover at table five. "See the guy eating the sandwich? The tall man in the yacht club clothes?"

Lila nodded. "Too overdone. Nobody's wearing epaulets this season."

Jessica rolled her eyes. "He's on an around-the-world sailing trip from Portugal! Isn't that romantic?"

"Peachy," Lila agreed, but she was watching the scruffy stranger again. "Well, you seem to have made an admirer out of that loser. His eyes are following your every move."

"How can you tell under that big hat?"

"A woman knows these things," Lila said, as if she

were thirty years old instead of sixteen. "I'm surprised your own guy radar didn't tell you."

"My own guy radar is set for gorgeous, hunky, *clean* guys! I just wish he'd leave so I could get some customers again."

"I thought that's what I was."

"Of course you are," Jessica said, remembering the tip. "What can I get for you?"

"The fruit plate, with yogurt," Lila decided. "So are you still meeting your television intern this afternoon?"

Jessica smiled, thinking about Scott's sexy blue eyes. "I'm off at two o'clock, and I'm meeting him at four. That'll give me time to shower and change so I don't smell like french fries."

Lila grimaced. "How is your high-and-mighty sister taking the news about him?"

"Well—"

"I can't imagine Elizabeth would approve. Didn't she warn you off older men after that fiasco with Jeremy Randall? I mean, you did go after another woman's fiancé."

"That wasn't the way it was, and you know it!" Jessica insisted. "Besides, this is completely different. Scott's not engaged to anyone. And he's not that much older than we are!"

"How old is he, anyway?"

"I'm not sure," Jessica admitted. "He looks about twenty. And what my snoopy sister doesn't know won't hurt her. So keep quiet about him."

"My lips are sealed," Lila said.

Jessica sighed. "When I'm a famous television star, I'll be able to date him openly, no matter how old he is. Nobody will dare criticize me."

"I'll keep that in mind when you're a famous television star," Lila said, eyeing Jessica's apron with an air of disdain. "Until then, I assume you won't want to be seen with Scott in too public a place—at least, not in any place where there might be people who would mention it to Elizabeth. Or to Ken."

"True. But sneaking around can be fun. It kind of makes romance more exciting."

"So where are you meeting Prince Charming today?"

"In the school parking lot."

Lila wrinkled her nose. "He sure knows how to show a date a good time. Obviously he's sparing no expense."

"I told you last night. He's scouting locations for a miniseries about a southern California high school. If he recommends that they film it here, it could be my big break!"

"Just because he's looking for a California high school doesn't necessarily mean you'll end up starring in the miniseries."

"No," Jessica acknowledged. "But you never know. If he really likes me, then he just might drop a few hints to Jillian DeRiggi, the producer. And when she sees me, well, who knows? Maybe she'll think I'm perfect for a big, juicy role!"

"And maybe she won't."

"It doesn't have to be a big part, of course.

Couldn't you just see me on television, in a small but pivotal role? I could play a girl who dies tragically in the first episode, leaving behind my grief-stricken friends and throwing the whole school into turmoil. Or I could be the beautiful but untouchable girl that every boy in school worships from afar but is afraid to ask out. Or I could be—"

Lila cut in. "Or you could be the teenage waitress who gets fired from her job for hanging out with me when she's supposed to be working."

Jessica followed Lila's eyes. Mr. Jenkins was standing behind the counter, glaring expectantly at Jessica.

"Oops," Jessica said. "It's a good thing he's having so much trouble telling Elizabeth and me apart. It comes in handy when he's mad about something!"

Before Jessica slipped through the door of the storage room, she turned one last time to check on her customers. Unfortunately the guy in the floppy hat still seemed to be staring straight at her.

The door to the storage room swung open, and Elizabeth nearly crashed into her sister. Jessica was emerging from the room with a penitent expression on her face.

"Whew! Am I glad that's over!" Jessica breathed. "Jenkins was chewing me out for 'not providing excellent service.' He said I was talking to Lila for too long when I should have been serving other customers."

"He was probably right," Elizabeth told her. She

fitted a new filter into the coffeemaker. "Face it, Jess. You lose track of time when you're gossiping with your friends."

"That's almost exactly what he said," Jessica told her. She grinned. "Except that when he said it, he called me Elizabeth."

Elizabeth's mouth dropped open. "And you let him go on thinking it was *me* who was goofing off instead of working?"

"Don't worry about it. It'll be good for your reputation. If you can't be truly wild and crazy, you can at least let people think you are."

"Talking to Lila is hardly a walk on the wild side," Elizabeth said, flicking the switch on the coffeemaker. "Maybe you should get back out to your customers before Mr. Jenkins sees you again and *I* get into even more trouble."

Jessica shook her head. "What customers? Nobody will sit in my section with that filthy, disgusting-looking creep there."

Elizabeth shuddered. "That guy really makes me nervous. Every time I'm in the dining room, I can feel him watching me."

"Me too. He won't stop staring. Yuck!"

"Maybe it's our imagination," Elizabeth suggested, not really believing it. "I wonder if Jane thinks he's staring at her too."

"Nope on both counts," Jessica told her. "In fact, both Jane and Lila said they noticed that he was staring at *me*. Maybe he just likes blondes. Or maybe he thinks we're one person."

"I don't think so, Jessica. I'm not sure how I can tell, but I've got a very strange feeling about that man."

Elizabeth stood behind the counter of the Marina Café that afternoon, wrapping silverware in cloth napkins. Jane appeared from the kitchen with a tray. At the same time, Jessica walked up from the dining room, pocketing her latest tip.

"Is it two o'clock yet?" Jessica asked. "My feet are killing me."

"Five minutes after," Elizabeth said with a grin. "That's what you get for not wearing a watch of your own."

"Hallelujah!" Jessica cried. "I can't wait to get home and take a shower so I can—" She stopped suddenly.

"So you can what?" Elizabeth asked. "You never told me why you're leaving early this afternoon. What is it this time, an emergency trip to the mall with Lila?"

Jessica nodded vigorously. "That's exactly it. Lila's going to help me pick out a bikini." She untied her apron. "Well, guys, I'm outta here as soon as I grab something to drink. I promise I'll think about you two slaving away while I'm having fun this afternoon."

Elizabeth smiled. "Actually, it's been a really good day so far. I think I'll manage a few more hours."

Jessica poured herself half a glass of diet soda and drank it down in one gulp. "At least that spooky guy in the gross clothes finally left."

"Not completely," Jane said. "I noticed him on my break. He's out on the dock, fishing. But he really seems to be watching this place—probably hoping for another glimpse of you two." She grinned wickedly. "This guy's got it bad for you girls. It must be true love."

"Gag!" Jessica called over her shoulder as she practically sprinted toward the door. "Thanks for the warning. I'll stay away from the dock. Happy wait-ressing!"

A minute later Elizabeth was once again alone with the silverware. She gazed across the café. The dining room was striped with yellow bars of sunlight from the huge windows. Outside, white sails gleamed against a turquoise sky. For the hundredth time that day, Elizabeth found herself daydreaming. She saw herself balanced on the deck of one of those lovely sailboats, with the sun warm on her face. The boat bounced gently over the swells, and the ocean's surface reflected the clear blue sky and the golden sunlight. And she wasn't alone on the boat. Standing beside her, adjusting a sail, was a young man wearing a navy windbreaker, his wavy, light brown hair tossed by the wind. . . .

Moments later, Elizabeth's eyes widened. The door of the restaurant had opened, and in walked the guy from the Dairi Burger, as if Elizabeth's fantasy had conjured him up. She dropped a set of silverware with a clatter.

Jane returned to the counter. "Check out that guy," she said, nudging Elizabeth. "He can climb in my rigging anytime!"

Elizabeth couldn't stop staring at his handsome face. She'd never believed in fate before, but his timing was too perfect to be coincidence. *Maybe we are soul mates.*

"Well, what are you waiting for?" Jane asked. "That's your table, isn't it?"

Elizabeth took a deep breath and hurried out to take his order.

"What can I get for you?" she asked, her heart pounding in her chest.

"I'll have an iced coffee with half-and-half," the young man said. "With three sugars and a straw."

Elizabeth's mouth dropped open.

"Is something wrong?" he asked. His deep blue eyes were sweetly soft in his tanned face. They had tiny wrinkles at their edges, as if he'd been squinting into the wind.

"Oh, no," Elizabeth said quickly. "Everything's just fine." She walked quickly from the dining room.

"What a hunk!" Jane exclaimed in the kitchen a few minutes later. "And you should see his boat!"

Elizabeth looked at her curiously. "He only just walked in. How do you know he has a boat?"

Jane shrugged. "If there's one thing you learn in college, it's how to do efficient research. Trina, the dishwasher, says she talked to your newest customer out on the docks this morning. She told me which boat was his, and I slipped out a minute ago to take a look."

Elizabeth was still shaking because her dream guy had ordered "her" drink. She fixed the iced coffee quickly and hurried back to the dining room with it. He was still there, now writing in his spiral-bound notebook.

He looked up when she set the coffee in front of him. "Thanks." His smile was heart-stopping.

"Will there be anything else?"

"No, that's all for today."

Elizabeth ran into Jane in the storage room a few minutes later. "Tell me more," she begged. "What kind of boat does he have?"

"It's a forty-foot sloop named the *Emily Dickinson*."

Elizabeth felt faint. Emily Dickinson was her very favorite poet. "Did you happen to get the name of the guy, too—or just the name of the boat?"

Jane shrugged. "Sorry. My research methods aren't that thorough. Trina couldn't remember his name. But get this—he's just sailed in from Hawaii, all by himself. Now he's on his way to South America."

"What else did Trina say?"

"Not much. Just that he's some sort of writer."

"*A writer?*" Elizabeth was having trouble catching her breath. One little thought about soul mates the night before and this guy seemed to drop down from heaven, just for her.

"Don't just stand there, sweetie," Jane told her. "You're dying to know more, aren't you? So march yourself back out there and strike up a conversation."

Elizabeth nodded. Jane was absolutely right. She wheeled around and headed back to the dining room.

When she reached the young writer's table, her heart sank. He was gone.

But she smiled when she saw that he'd left her a twenty-five-percent tip. Somehow, she was sure they'd meet again.

"So this is the famous Sweet Valley High," Scott Maderlake said as he climbed out of his red Miata. "I can already see that it's got a lot of potential—it's very California. The visuals are great."

Jessica saw the way his blue eyes slid over her swingy yellow halter dress. He was definitely talking about more than the high school. *Lila Fowler, eat your heart out. Yellow looks terrific on some people.*

Scott had a speculative look on his face. "It looks like the kind of place where a lot of exciting things might happen."

"I could tell you some pretty intense stories!" Jessica said. "Wilder than anything your scriptwriters could dream up, I guarantee."

"How about telling me over an early dinner?" Scott asked. "It's obvious that we can't get inside the school right now, though I'd like to eventually."

"Give me a few days," Jessica said. "I'll think of a way to get you in."

"Great!" Scott said, with a sexy smile that made Jessica's knees melt. "For now, why don't you leave your Jeep here and come with me in the Miata? You suggest a place to eat, and you can show me the sights along the way."

Jessica nodded eagerly. "Sounds like a plan."

"Can you recommend a restaurant up the coast?"

Jessica slid into the front seat of his car and thought for a moment. She wondered if it would be rude to suggest Café Mirabeau, one of the most expensive restaurants in the area. She took in the airplanelike control panel, the soft leather interior, and the solid wood dashboard. *He can afford it,* she decided.

Mr. Wakefield pulled his brown LTD into the driveway of the Wakefield house on Calico Drive. "Good," he breathed. "I'm the first one home." He wanted to make sure nobody reached the mailbox before he did—just in case John Marin had made any new deliveries.

He ran to box and yanked the day's mail out of it. Then he quickly flipped through the envelopes and catalogs. "Thank goodness!" he said with a sigh. "Nothing out of the ordinary. I guess Marin decided to lay low for the day."

Prince Albert barked a greeting as Mr. Wakefield stepped into the house. Mr. Wakefield walked through the downstairs, his gaze sliding around the familiar rooms. Then he collapsed onto the living room couch, patting Prince Albert's head. "It's all right, Albert," he said. "There's no sign of an intruder. I don't think Marin's been here today."

The dog barked a cheerful reply.

"You're right," Mr. Wakefield said. "I probably overreacted. Maybe I shouldn't have called a private investigator. But if the police can't protect my family,

I have to take things into my own hands."

Then his heart skipped a beat. A sheet of lined paper lay on the coffee table, with writing on it. "What's that?" he said aloud. The golden retriever stared at him quizzically.

Ned lifted the note from the table, barely breathing. Had he been wrong? Had Marin been in the house that day after all? Was the note another threat?

Yo, Mom and Dad, the note said in Jessica's loopy scrawl. *I'm with Lila. Don't expect me for dinner. See ya later tonight. P.S. Chill out, Dad! You worry too much.*

Mr. Wakefield exhaled, relieved that the note wasn't from Marin. At the same time, he was concerned about Jessica. Did she really have to go out every single night?

Prince Albert nudged the note out of the way and licked his hand. "You're right, boy," Mr. Wakefield said. "I'm getting paranoid again. But I'm not sorry I called Battaglia. You can never be too careful."

Chapter 7

"So Winston Egbert, the nerdiest kid in the junior class, was left with his neighbor's baby girl for a whole week!" Jessica related to Scott over dessert at Café Mirabeau.

Scott was hanging on her every word. "So what does a sixteen-year-old guy do with an abandoned baby when his own parents are on vacation?"

Jessica's lips slid over a spoonful of chocolate mousse. She'd certainly outdone herself on the choice of restaurant. Dinner had been terrific, the mousse was the best she'd ever tasted, and Scott hadn't even winced at the prices on the menu.

She gestured with her spoon. "For one thing, Winston the Nerd became the most popular guy in the class. Crowds of girls showed up at his house every day to play with the baby." She laughed. "It was a good thing—he really needed the help. I've never seen anything as funny as

Winston Egbert trying to diaper a baby!"

"What about school?" Scott asked. "Did he stay out the whole week?"

"Oh, no," Jessica said. "He brought little Daisy with him, and we all took turns watching her during our free periods. You should've seen us, passing her off like a football, hiding her from teachers—"

"That is priceless! You know, Jessica, you're right. These stories you're telling me are better than anything Hollywood has to offer. We could use you as a consultant on the miniseries. I mean, if you'd be interested."

Jessica froze with a spoonful of chocolate mousse halfway to her mouth. She could hardly believe what she'd just heard. A slow smile spread across her face. "If I'd be interested? Are you kidding? I'd love it! But Scott, you ain't heard nothing yet. Let me tell you about the time my sister's best friend, Enid Rollins, was in a plane crash. . . ."

Elizabeth sat at the Dairi Burger with Enid that night. Her friend was talking, but Elizabeth's eyes kept straying to the corner booth where *he* had sat the night before.

She had been relieved when Todd said he'd be busy tonight. For a change of pace, he'd said, he was going to a drag race with some of the other guys from the school basketball team. A drag race! That was supposed to be exciting?

Of course I love Todd, she reminded herself. *But right now, a little distance from him is just what I need.*

"I can't wait to meet Jane," Enid was saying. "You did say she'd be here at eight o'clock, right?"

Elizabeth shook her head, trying to clear it. "I'm sorry, Enid. What was that?"

Enid took a sip of her diet soda. "What's up with you, Liz? You seem like you're a million miles away. Is everything all right?"

Elizabeth opened her mouth to tell Enid about the good-looking young stranger she couldn't get out of her mind. But suddenly there was a hand on her shoulder. She whirled around, half expecting to see her mystery man.

"Hey, Liz!" Jane said. "Sorry I'm a little late."

Elizabeth introduced her new friend to Enid, then slid over in the booth so that Jane could sit down.

"So, are you still obsessing about Sailor Boy?" Jane asked.

Elizabeth nodded sheepishly. "I can't stop thinking about him. I feel like we were meant to be together, but I don't even know his name."

Enid's eyes widened. "What in the world are you talking about?"

"I was just going to tell you about it. There's this guy I saw in here last night, when I was with Todd. It sounds weird, but we looked at each other across the room, and, I don't know. We connected."

"But you didn't even talk to him?"

Elizabeth shrugged. "Not last night. But he came into the café today—and Enid, it's like we're soul mates."

"I thought you and Todd were soul mates!"

"I don't know what to think about Todd. He's driving me crazy lately. We've been together for so long. And suddenly I'm bored. I want something . . . *different*."

"A different guy?"

"A different life! I'd love it if Todd could help me find what I'm looking for. But he doesn't understand, and he won't even try. He acts like I'm a spoiled kid who doesn't know how good I've got it." She bit her lip. "Sometimes I wonder if he's right."

Enid shook her head. "Of course he's not right. There's nothing wrong with wanting to expand your horizons. Todd should be more supportive."

Jane whistled. "You ought to see this sailor, Enid," she said in a conspiratorial tone. "He's gorgeous! And his sailboat may be even better looking than he is."

Enid stared at Elizabeth. "His sailboat?"

"Yeah, he owns a sailboat," Elizabeth said. "But Enid, it gets worse."

"How can it be worse?"

"His boat's named the *Emily Dickinson*—and he's a writer!"

"Oh, boy," Enid said, her forehead wrinkling with concern. "This is serious. This guy really does sound like your soul mate."

"What's so wrong with that?" Jane asked them both. "I say go with the flow."

Enid raised her eyebrows. "Elizabeth, I'm worried that you're going to do something you'll regret. As you just said, you and Todd have been together for a long time. Is this mystery guy of yours worth screwing up that relationship for?"

"I don't know. I just don't know."

"You sound pretty mixed up, kid," Jane said, patting her on the arm. "You're never going to know for sure until you have a conversation with Mr. Sailor that amounts to more than 'Will that be one sugar in your coffee, or two?'"

"Three, actually," Elizabeth said. She absentmindedly stirred her iced coffee with her straw.

Jane gave her a blank look. "Come again?"

Elizabeth sighed. "Never mind. It's not important."

"So what're you going to do?" Enid asked, looking at her expectantly.

"There's really nothing I can do until I actually meet this guy. I guess I'll just keep my eyes open and hope that he comes back into the café."

"Maybe he won't," Jane pointed out. "For all we know, he could be casting off for South America as we speak."

"He'll be back," Elizabeth said quietly. "I'm sure of it."

Jessica lay on her rumpled bed that night, twisting the telephone cord around her finger. "And then, Lila, he said that he could use me as a consultant on the miniseries! Can you believe it?"

Lila's bored skepticism oozed through the phone line. "Is he going to pay you?"

"Is getting paid the only thing you ever think

about?" Jessica cried. "The money isn't what's important!"

"Bite your tongue!"

"Lila, think about the opportunity! The closer I am to the production of the miniseries, the more likely I am to get cast in it. Don't you see?"

"I just can't take this very seriously, Jess. For your entire life, every two weeks you've been finding a new, surefire way to become a star."

"This is different!" Jessica said, jumping to her feet.

"You always say that!"

"You wait and see. Scott's so psyched about the stories I've been telling him that he might just convince the producer to use them in the plot. And if they've got a story line about Jessica Wakefield, why should they go any further than me to find the perfect woman for the role?"

Jessica sucked in her cheeks and watched herself in the mirror, trying to decide if she looked more glamorous that way. "So, Lila. What do you think I should wear to the Emmy Awards—something black and slinky?"

Lila's resigned sigh crackled through the phone. "I'll tell you what, Jess. You win an Emmy, and I'll let you have your pick of anything in my closet."

"Thanks, Li. And I'll be sure to thank you in my acceptance speech." She lifted her long hair off her neck to see what it would look like piled on top of her head. Suddenly she dropped it and put her hand to her mouth. "Oh, no!"

"What's wrong?" Lila asked. "Has your show been canceled already?"

"My necklace is gone! My gold lavaliere necklace, just like Elizabeth's."

"It's probably tangled up in your jewelry box."

"No, Lila. It's not. You know I hardly ever take it off. I'm sure I was wearing it earlier this evening."

"So what's the big deal? It couldn't be worth all that much. It's only fourteen karat."

"It's not the money! My parents gave us those necklaces on our sixteenth birthday. And my mom had a fit last week when I lost a bracelet my grandmother sent. She'll go ballistic if I tell her I lost the necklace too."

"Then you'll just have to find it before she notices."

Wednesday morning at the Marina Café was hectic. After a couple of hours of racing back and forth between the kitchen and the dining room, Elizabeth darted into the storage room; Mr. Jenkins had sent her back for paper towels to fill the dispenser in the ladies' room. She was determined to find the towels quickly so she could get back to the dining room and collect more tips.

Unfortunately the storage room was a mess. Elizabeth finally spotted a cardboard box marked PAPER TOWELS, but it was blocked by a half-dozen other crates. She'd have to dig her way down to it, one box at a time.

"Darn! I'll never get back to the customers at this

rate," she muttered as she began hoisting boxes. "Why did Jenkins have to pick me?"

A few minutes later she finally reached the paper towels. As she lifted the box, she tensed. All of a sudden, the tiny hairs on the back of her neck stood up straight. Someone else was in the storage room.

She dropped the box and spun around. The scary-looking guy from the dock stood facing her, still wearing the enormous hat that concealed his eyes. Up close, he looked positively sinister, especially now that she was alone with him.

"What are you doing here?" she demanded in a choked whisper.

Before she finished getting out the words, the man had disappeared.

Tears of fright blurred Elizabeth's vision as she tore open the box of paper towels and jerked out a package. She gulped for air. Then she raced out of the storage room.

As Elizabeth emerged into the dining room she collided with a tall, strong man. She nearly screamed.

"Hey, hey! It's all right," said a deep voice. Elizabeth looked up into the blue eyes of her soul mate.

She felt her face turning pink with embarrassment; he practically had his arms around her. She pulled away and tried to collect herself. "I'm sorry for crashing into you," she said finally. "There was just this man in the storage room who gave me the creeps, and I thought . . ."

"You look really rattled," he said in a soothing

voice. "Why don't you take a break, and we'll go outside for a few minutes. Some fresh air will do you good."

Elizabeth nodded. He was right—she was too frazzled to wait on customers. "Give me a minute to get someone to cover for me," she said, scanning the dining room for Jessica. "I'll see if my sister can watch my tables."

Jessica turned to the door of the kitchen in surprise. Elizabeth had just run in as if she were being chased. Her face was flushed, and her blue eyes were wide. She seemed out of breath.

"What's with you?" Jessica asked, making a peanut-butter sandwich for the around-the-world sailor from Portugal. He'd shown up again for breakfast.

Elizabeth scanned the kitchen, panting. "Good, Mr. Jenkins isn't in here."

"He's out back arguing with a seafood distributor," Jessica said, gesturing toward the back door. "Why? What's wrong?"

Elizabeth shook her head. "Nothing's wrong," she said unconvincingly. "But Jess, I need to go outside for a few minutes. Will you cover my tables?"

"No way! I've got enough work to do of my own without yours too. Ask Jane to do it."

"Please, Jessica. If *you* cover for me, Mr. Jenkins won't notice I'm gone. He'll think you're both of us. I'll be back in ten minutes, I swear."

"I'll do it on one condition," Jessica said, putting the peanut butter back on the shelf.

"What?"

"I need to leave a few hours early. I have some, uh, things to get done. I'm going shopping with Lila this afternoon. There's, uh, a fashion show at the mall at three o'clock. I'll cover for you now, but you have to cover for me then."

"You work for me for ten *minutes,* and then I cover for you for a few *hours?* That's not fair!"

Jessica shrugged. "OK, so take twenty minutes."

Elizabeth sighed, quickly untying her apron and throwing it over a hook. "All right, all right. It's a deal."

"And I want half the tips from any of your customers that I wait on!"

"That's extortion!"

Jessica smiled. "I prefer to think of it as private enterprise."

"Jessica!"

"OK, OK. No tips."

"Thanks, Jess. You're the best." Elizabeth thrust a package of paper towels into her sister's hands. "And put this in the ladies' room when you get a chance."

"Wait a minute! You still haven't told me where you're going!" Jessica protested.

But Elizabeth was already gone.

Halyards clanged in the breeze as Elizabeth walked along the docks of the marina with the sailor. His name, she'd finally learned, was Ben Morgan.

Ben touched her arm. "You're still shaking."

"I know," Elizabeth said. "It's kind of embarrassing. But that guy really freaked me out. Only restaurant employees are supposed to be in the storage room. And he was so seedy looking . . . ugh." She shook her head. "Let's talk about something else. Tell me about yourself."

Ben smiled, and Elizabeth felt breathless all over again. "Well," he said, "I've just spent a month 'on this wondrous sea, sailing silently.'"

"That's Emily Dickinson you just quoted!"

"Guilty as charged," Ben said. "Sorry. I'm kind of a poetry fanatic. Sometimes I forget that I shouldn't inflict my habit on others."

"I'm the same way," Elizabeth said. "And Emily Dickinson is my favorite!"

"No kidding? What a coincidence. I even named my boat after her!"

"Really?" Elizabeth asked, trying to sound surprised.

Ben smiled again. "A man gets a little strange sailing around by himself, with only reading and writing for company."

"Writing? What do you write?"

"Well, I'm working on a novel right now. It's a travel-adventure story. I'm taking a year off from college to sail around and collect information for it."

Elizabeth's heart pounded. "How wonderful," she breathed. "That is exactly what I'd like to do, if I weren't so . . . hemmed in."

Ben stopped walking. He turned to face her. "Hemmed in by what, Elizabeth?"

She shook her head. "By Sweet Valley,

97

California, I guess. By being Elizabeth Wakefield."

"I don't understand."

Elizabeth laughed. "I'm not sure I do either. It's just that everyone has all these expectations of me. I'm supposed to be a good little girl, and get good grades, and listen to my parents. And mostly I just go along with all those expectations."

Ben nodded. "I know what you mean. It's like your life is all scripted out, and you're just playing along. You're desperate to do something . . . unexpected."

Elizabeth stared into his beautiful dark blue eyes. She felt as if she could fall into those eyes as easily as she could fall off the edge of the dock and into the sparkling water below. "Yes!" she cried, startled to hear him express her own feelings. "That's it. That's it exactly!"

Suddenly Elizabeth felt embarrassed. After all, this guy was a complete stranger. "Look, I want to thank you for being so nice to me. But I'm rambling. I can't help it; you're very easy to talk to. Thanks for saving me from that creep in the storage room. But I should get back to work."

She turned and fled toward the restaurant. She could feel Ben's gorgeous blue eyes on her back, and she desperately wanted to reverse her direction and run straight back—right into his arms.

Calico Drive looked deserted this late in the morning. John Marin pulled his car to a halt in front of the Wakefield house and reached for the small, tissue-wrapped bundle on the seat beside him. He stuffed the bundle into a padded envelope and scrawled *Ned* across the front.

Then he flipped down the window visor to reveal a picture of Ned Wakefield he'd clipped there.

"Counselor, I'm holding you in contempt," he sneered at the photograph. "And your sentence will be torture."

Marin sealed the envelope. Then he leaped from the car and slid the package into the Wakefields' mailbox.

For a moment he stopped on the sidewalk and stared at the quiet house. "I wish I could stay here and wait for you, Counselor," he said, his eyes narrowed into hard slits. "I'd love to see your face when you open that package. Aw, Ned, you're so much fun to torment. It's almost too easy!" He laughed as he climbed back into the car.

"A private investigator? Really! Battaglia's a novice compared to me. He hasn't even slowed me down. I could have stuck a knife into either of those sweet young girls by now, and Battaglia too. But I'm having so much fun, keeping you on your toes, Ned. I'd like to prolong the agony just a little bit longer."

He laughed again, gunned the engine, and drove off down the street. "Besides, I can't decide which twin is prettier, Jessica or Elizabeth. Which one should I kill first, Counselor? Which one?"

Chapter 8

Elizabeth stepped warily into the café, her heart racing. She felt exhilarated by her walk along the docks with Ben. On the other hand, she expected Jessica to pounce on her any minute, demanding to know where she'd been.

She breathed a relieved sigh when she saw that Jessica had her hands full with a birthday party at table five. A half-dozen six-year-olds were arguing over a pile of paper party hats while three adults tried in vain to referee. Obviously it would be some time before Jessica got around to asking about Elizabeth's absence.

Elizabeth waved a hand at her sister to signal that she was back on duty. Jessica threw her a dirty look, taking her attention away from the table just long enough for a chubby boy to dump a glass of grape juice down the front of her shirt. Elizabeth tried to stifle her laughter. On Jessica's list of favorite things, baby-sitting ranked somewhere between algebra tests and zits.

Jane accosted her as soon as she ran back to the kitchen to grab her apron. "So tell me about Sailor Boy!"

Elizabeth felt her face coloring. She smiled weakly. "Sorry, I've got a ton of customers to serve. I'll fill you in later."

Breakfast time melted into lunch hour, and business in the café never let up. Elizabeth hardly had time to catch her breath between customers. She was happy about the volume of business. Most of the customers were pleasant and interesting. And after two days of waitressing, Elizabeth was beginning to feel in control of the job. She loved the sense of competence that came with knowing what to do and what to say. By noon she could juggle orders at five different tables at once without mixing anything up.

"I'm really getting the hang of this!" she whispered to Jane once as they slid by each other, trays held high.

Jane smiled. "I knew you would."

Waitressing took her mind off her scare in the storage room that morning. Already it seemed like a dream. Elizabeth could almost believe she'd imagined the whole incident.

But she couldn't keep her mind off Ben. Every time Elizabeth glanced out the expanse of windows—toward the sailboats bobbing in their berths—she could feel tropical breezes in her hair and see the white beaches and rugged volcanic peaks of Hawaii off the bow. In her daydreams, it was always Ben who stood beside her on the deck. Every time the bell on the door jingled, she looked up. She'd love to see Ben saunter in for iced coffee, his light brown hair disheveled by the ocean breeze.

A little after noon, Jessica left for the day. Elizabeth was preparing a salad in the kitchen when Jane stopped behind her and sang into her ear, "Lover boy's arrived!"

Elizabeth's heart jumped. She smoothed her hair and took a deep breath. Then she checked the coffeepot to make sure there was plenty in it for Ben's iced coffee. Then, grinning, she walked steadily through the swinging door to meet him.

"How's my favorite waitress?" asked a sexy voice from the counter.

Elizabeth exhaled slowly, disappointed. Todd leaned across the counter and kissed her on the cheek. "Gimme a nice cold root beer!"

Mr. Wakefield couldn't stand it any longer. He'd been sitting at his desk for half the day, going over Marianna's briefs for the *West Coast Oilcam* wrongful-dismissal case. But he couldn't keep his mind on his work. The only wrongful dismissal that interested him lately was John Marin's early release from prison.

He grabbed the telephone and dialed James Battaglia's number. "Jim? It's Ned. What have you got for me?"

"Not much," the private investigator said. "This Marin guy knows how to cover his tracks."

"Have you been able to locate him?"

"I'm sure he's nearby. But every time I think I've almost caught up with him, he throws me a curveball. I get the feeling he's toying with me."

Mr. Wakefield nodded. "That sounds like Marin."

"Have the girls noticed anyone unusual hanging around?"

"They haven't mentioned anything odd. Has your man been keeping an eye on them during the day?"

"Yeah, he's been down near the marina as much as possible, watching the café. I've dropped by the neighborhood myself a few times, in between trying to track down Marin. So far, neither of us has seen anything suspicious. Have you told the twins what to watch for?"

Mr. Wakefield shook his head. "No. They don't know anything about Marin. Until I've got more to go on, upsetting my daughters isn't going to do any good."

"All right, Ned. I'll play it any way you want."

"Have you been in touch with the police? Did you get Marin's picture from them?"

"I'm in constant contact with Detective Cabrini. And a courier dropped the mug shot by my office yesterday. I gave a copy to my hired man last night so he can watch for him at the marina. Funny, Marin doesn't look at all like you described him. You said he has a baby face and could almost pass as a teenager. I thought he looked about thirty in the photo."

Mr. Wakefield shrugged. "Well, the man's twenty-eight years old now. The last picture I've seen was taken years ago. Cabrini must have sent you something more recent."

"I guess doing time in the state pen would age anybody."

"Do the police have any new information on his whereabouts?"

"Nothing substantial. But Cabrini and I will coordinate our efforts if either of us gets a lead."

"Good," Mr. Wakefield said, but he felt a sinking sensation in the pit of his stomach. "Keep me informed, Jim."

Mr. Wakefield slammed down the receiver and jumped up from his desk. He threw the *Oilcam* papers into his briefcase, grabbed his suit jacket from the back of his chair, and stalked out of the room. "Trudy, I'm leaving early," he barked as he passed the office manager. "There's something I have to check on at home."

A half hour later he sat at his desk at home, turning a brown, padded envelope over and over in his hands. *Ned* was scribbled across the front in a large, angular hand. There was no return address, but Mr. Wakefield knew instantly who had sent it. He tore open the package. With shaking hands, he unwrapped a tissue-paper bundle.

Such a lovely young neck, the note said.

A gold lavaliere necklace fell to the desk, its chain jingling softly, like a young girl's quiet laughter.

Jessica could barely stop laughing long enough to give instructions to Scott. "Boost me up a little higher," she urged. "I can almost climb in." Her head and shoulders were inside the window of the girls' locker room at Sweet Valley High, but the rest of her was still outside. The windowsill was cutting into her solar plexus, and the cradle of Scott's hands felt wobbly through the sole of her left sneaker. The whole scene was hysterically funny.

Suddenly Jessica stopped laughing. "Shhh!" she hissed. "I think I heard something!"

"Inside the building?"

"No, back toward the parking lot. Oh, my gosh. We're going to get caught. Did you hear anything?"

"Not a thing."

Jessica remained still for as long as she could, balanced in the window. Finally she shook her head. "Maybe it was my imagination."

"Somehow I can tell you have an active one," Scott said. "Can you pull yourself in now?" He lifted her foot a little higher. "I can't keep you up in the air like this forever."

"Yep. That'll do it. I think I can make it now." She pulled herself into a crouch in the windowsill and then jumped to the tile floor of the locker room. Even in the summer the smells of sweaty gym socks, deodorant, and cosmetics blended into a heady aroma.

"Are you all right?" Scott called from outside.

"Piece of cake!" Jessica yelled back. "Come around the corner of the building and I'll let you in the back way."

"I can't believe we're really doing this," Scott said

after she'd opened the back door of the locker room for him. "You don't seem like the breaking-and-entering type."

"I didn't break a thing," Jessica said with mock indignity. "I only entered! The lock on that window's been broken for two years."

Scott dusted his hands off on his navy windbreaker. "I take it you've had occasion to use that entrance before."

Jessica shrugged. "Remind me to tell you about it sometime. You might be able to use it in your miniseries."

"We might be able to use *this* in the miniseries. But I don't know how I'll explain it to Jillian if she has to come bail me out of jail for breaking into this place."

"Just tell her you wanted your research to be thorough."

Scott shook his head. "Jessica, you're unbelievable. So, is this what the inside of a girls' locker room looks like? When I was in high school, I spent a lot of long, boring math classes dreaming about getting inside one of these places."

Jessica laughed. "Well, I hope it's everything you dreamed it would be."

"Actually, it looks just like the guys' locker room. But it smells better."

"Ugh," Jessica said with a grimace. "Hey, here's a good story for you. Do you see that football helmet and protective gear back in that storage area?"

"Yeah. What's it doing here?"

"Claire Middleton," Jessica said, as if the name explained everything. "She's a junior here, the first girl in the district to play on the boys' varsity football team. She tried out for first-string quarterback early in the year and came pretty close to making it. Now she plays second string."

"A girl playing quarterback? You're pulling my leg."

"That's what we all thought when we heard she was trying out. But she turned out to be just as good as the guys. Almost as good as Ken—" She stopped, reluctant to discuss her boyfriend around Scott.

"Ken who?"

"Uh, Ken Matthews. He's the first-string quarterback. Come on, the smell in here is choking me. Let me show you the rest of the school."

Scott shrugged. "Sure. Why not? As long as we're already trespassing, we might as well get the whole tour."

Elizabeth smiled when her best friend walked into the Marina Café that afternoon. "Enid!" she called. "I'm glad you could stop by."

"Which is your section?" Enid asked. "I wouldn't want my hard-earned tip money going to any other waitress."

"Thanks! I need all the help I can get if I'm going to win the big tip contest," she said.

"Then you should have chosen your friends better. Lila Fowler can afford to tip a lot better than I can. I think that gives Jessica the advantage."

"Maybe, but you're a much more generous person than Lila."

"Ha! So was Ebenezer Scrooge. I just saw Lila on the beach five minutes ago, arguing with a vendor about the price of a can of soda."

"That's funny. I could've sworn Jessica said she and Lila were going to a fashion show at the mall this afternoon." Elizabeth checked her watch. "Jessica should be there right about now, panting over clothes she can't afford."

"I hadn't heard about a fashion show. But believe me, I just left Lila on the beach not ten minutes ago."

Elizabeth shrugged. "Maybe I got the time wrong."

"Or maybe Jessica was using Lila as an alibi for one of her schemes." Enid raised an eyebrow.

"Well, I don't have time to worry about her schedule—especially since I'm covering her section as well as my own this afternoon. Speaking of which, what can I get you?"

Enid shook her head. "How about one of those iced coffees you've been raving about?" She grinned. "What is it, with half a sugar and three straws?"

"That's half-and-half, three sugars, and one straw," Elizabeth corrected her. "It's a never-fail recipe for breaking out of a rut."

"Will drinking it make a good-looking sailor miraculously appear and carry me onto his boat so we can sail off into the sunset together?"

"Sorry. I'm a waitress, not a fairy godmother."

"Good. I'd get seasick anyway. Seriously, has your mystery man been back?"

Elizabeth nodded. "This morning. We strolled out along the docks during my break. Oh, Enid! It was so Old World. You know, a real, old-fashioned *promenade* on the wharf, watching the sails billow in the breeze."

"Do you at least know his name now?"

"His name's Ben. And he's absolutely perfect! I couldn't have created a better match for me if I were writing it in a novel. Which, by the way, he's doing— writing a novel, I mean."

"I hate to rain on your promenade," Enid said. "But what are you going to do about Todd?"

Elizabeth frowned. "Todd was in here today, an hour after I left Ben on the docks. What a contrast! I mean, he barrels in, looking like such a . . . *high school guy.* He was full of stories about that drag race he went to last night. *A drag race!*"

Enid sighed. "I know. It can't compare with sailing around the Hawaiian Islands. Ben sounds so exotic."

Elizabeth nodded. "And Todd is just Todd."

"That used to be enough for you."

"I know. And maybe it will be again. Maybe I'm just going through a phase. Am I crazy to risk what I've got with Todd? I mean, I don't even know how long Ben will be in port! And he's still a complete stranger, really."

Enid opened her mouth to reply, but Mr. Jenkins appeared behind the counter and beckoned to

Elizabeth. "Elizabeth, I believe the order is ready for table nine," he said with a disapproving stare.

Elizabeth sighed. "What a time for him to finally get my name right," she whispered to Enid. Then she grinned. "Coming, Mr. Jenkins!" she called in a louder voice. "But I'm not Elizabeth. I'm Jessica!"

Jessica and Scott stopped outside the door of the high school auditorium. "Here's where we have assemblies and school plays and band concerts and stuff," she said, gesturing toward the door. She knew she was babbling, but Scott seemed endlessly amused by her anecdotes, so she figured she might as well keep him entertained.

"We've got a really great band—the Droids. See that poster for them on the bulletin board? Olivia Davidson designed it. She's a friend of my sister's, kind of an artsy type. Did I tell you how she met her boyfriend, Harry Minton?"

Scott smiled and held open the door for her. "No, I don't think I've heard that one."

"She had a painting in an art show, and an anonymous person offered to buy it if Olivia would speak at a stuffy-sounding arts foundation."

Scott nodded. "That sounds like a big honor for a high school student."

"Olivia thought so too," Jessica said with a laugh. "Only when she got to the place, she found out there wasn't any arts foundation. Harry made the whole thing up just to meet her."

Scott looked at her admiringly. "Is there any

square inch of this school that you don't have a story about?"

"The chess club room," Jessica said instantly. "I'm happy to say that I've never set foot in the place and never plan to."

"I don't blame you," Scott said, laughing. "I've always been nervous around people who like things as slow and complicated as chess."

"Exactly!" Jessica said with a nod. "It's amazing how much you and I have in common."

"So what about this room?" Scott asked. "We're standing in front of the stage. As naturally dramatic as you are, I'm sure you must have a story about it."

"At least a dozen," Jessica said cheerfully, happy for the chance to inform him about her acting experience. "I've been in a lot of plays in this room. A few months ago I was Lady Macbeth. But my understudy was a two-faced liar who sabotaged me and made me miss opening night."

"I hope you got to play the part eventually."

"Oh, sure. I did all the other performances, and I got rave reviews. But you should have seen Lila Fowler, my snobby millionaire friend, in that play! She was so ticked off at having to play an ugly old witch that she started adding her own lines to the script. Have you ever heard a cast member say 'Oh, gross!' onstage, in the middle of a Shakespeare performance?"

Scott laughed. "You and your friends are just too much, Jessica. I should be taking notes on all this for our scriptwriters."

"Don't worry about it," she said magnanimously. "I'll remember which stories you liked and tell them myself."

"I'm so glad you've agreed to help us out with this production. You're going to be a wonderful addition to the crew."

Suddenly the look in Scott's deep blue eyes grew serious. For the first time Jessica was acutely aware of how all alone they were in the big, empty school building. Scott smiled at her, and his sexy grin seemed to light up the dim, cavernous auditorium. Jessica's eyes caressed his broad shoulders and his strong, muscular body.

Scott leaned close to Jessica. He put a hand on Jessica's neck, pulling her close. She closed her eyes and began to relax into his arms.

Suddenly she felt a prickling at the back of her scalp. Jessica's eyes shot open. She spun around just in time to see a shadowy figure disappear through the auditorium door.

Chapter 9

The Wakefields had just sat down to dinner on Wednesday evening. Mrs. Wakefield was telling Elizabeth about the new kitchen in the mansion she was renovating, but Mr. Wakefield couldn't keep his mind on skylights, granite countertops, and ceramic tiles.

He reached into his pocket to feel the necklace he'd received in the mail. He knew that the twins wore their identical lavalieres almost all the time. His stomach lurched every time he thought about it. Marin must have been close enough to one of them to grab it away. But close enough to which one? He couldn't see a necklace on either Jessica or Elizabeth, but one of them could be wearing the gold chain under her blouse. He drummed his fingers on the table.

"Has either of you seen or spoken with anybody out of the ordinary recently?" he blurted, interrupting the conversation.

Elizabeth choked on her iced tea. Jessica glanced up quickly. Both twins recovered quickly. They glanced at each other. Then they turned to look at him, their lovely, heart-shaped faces completely blank.

Elizabeth struggled to swallow a gulp of iced tea. She wondered what her father was getting at. He couldn't know about Ben. Could he? The handsome young writer and sailor was certainly unusual. But she wouldn't dream of telling her family about him. At least, not until she had sorted out her feelings for Todd.

"Oops," she said, forcing a carefree smile. "I guess that tea went down the wrong pipe! No, I don't think I've talked with anyone unusual in the last few days— unless you mean all the interesting customers we get at the marina."

Her father scrutinized her face. "Are you sure?"

Elizabeth laughed. "Well, there *is* Mr. Jenkins, our boss. He's pretty weird. No matter how many times we tell him, he can't get our names straight. I've just resigned myself to answering to the name 'Jessica' for the rest of the summer."

Jessica raised her eyebrows. "You could do worse."

"So you haven't seen anyone doing anything strange lately?" Mr. Wakefield asked again, his eyes oddly intense on Elizabeth's face.

"Only you, Dad," Jessica pointed out. "You've got to admit, you've been acting like a total basket case all week."

Elizabeth briefly considered bringing up the scene in the storage room with the seedy-looking man. But now that she'd had time to think about it, the whole incident seemed surrealistic, almost as if she'd dreamed it. *Maybe I did dream it,* she told herself. Even if it had really happened, it probably didn't mean a thing. The poor man was probably a little unstable and just got lost.

In any case, her father was acting paranoid enough lately when it came to the twins. If she told him that a creepy, badly dressed man had bumbled into the storage room by mistake and frightened her, her father just might lock both girls in the house for the rest of the summer. And that would make it awfully hard to make good on her resolution to seek out excitement—and to see Ben again.

"What about you, Jessica?" Mr. Wakefield asked.

He won't give it up, Jessica thought. *What is with Dad this week?* She wondered if her father somehow knew about Scott, but she dismissed the idea immediately. She hadn't even told Elizabeth about him. Lila was the only person who knew about him, and her father wasn't in the habit of calling Lila for the latest gossip.

Jessica shrugged. "Sure, I've met strange people this week," she began glibly. "At the café the other day I waited on a man who started in Portugal and is sailing around the world! He said he'll be in town for a week or so to rest. The same guy was in again today. Both times he ordered a peanut-butter sandwich for breakfast! That seemed pretty geeky for someone who's sailing around the world."

"Anything else?"

Jessica thought about the glimpse she'd caught of a mysterious person in the doorway of the school auditorium.

Sure, she said to herself. *And what would I say to Dad about that? "Oh, yeah, Dad. I climbed in the window of the girls' locker room at school so I could let this twenty-year-old television guy into the building. And then, right when he was about to kiss me . . ."*

Jessica noticed that her father was drumming his fingers on the table. He stared intently from one twin to the other. "You girls aren't hiding anything from me, are you?"

"No, Dad," they answered together.

Mrs. Wakefield looked concerned. "Ned, is there something in particular you're getting at?"

"No, no, nothing at all," he insisted. "I'm just making conversation."

Jessica glanced at Elizabeth and rolled her eyes in Mr. Wakefield's direction. Elizabeth looked away quickly. Jessica studied her sister's face, curious. Elizabeth was definitely hiding something.

Jim Battaglia's voice sounded tired over the phone that night. "Calm down, Ned," he urged. "You said the package had a necklace in it that belongs to one of your girls? Are you sure it's theirs and not just something similar he bought to scare you?"

"Positive. And that note he sent—" He broke off,

shaking his head. "What have you found, Jim? Has anyone out of the ordinary been close to either of my daughters?"

"I wasn't sure if I should mention it, Ned, but Jessica—"

"What is it, Jim? Has somebody suspicious been near her?"

"No, nothing like that. This really isn't what I was hired to find out, but Jessica seems to be seeing some guy she met at the café. I'm sure it's harmless. I sneaked a look at him myself this afternoon. I was at a bit of a distance, and it was dark. But I could tell that the guy wasn't Marin."

"So who is he?"

"I can find more out if you want me to. But since it's not Marin, I don't think it's relevant to this case."

"Do you know anything at all about him?"

"A little. You know that I hired a man to keep an eye on your daughters. I didn't want him to attract their attention or Marin's. So I had him dress inconspicuously, like the kind of local color that you find around any marina."

"What does this have to do with Jessica seeing some boy I don't know?"

"My man was in the café Tuesday and overheard Jessica telling her friend Lila that the new boyfriend's name is Scott. He's an intern with a television production company."

"I wonder why she never mentioned him at home."

"Lila wondered too." Battaglia spoke as if he was

117

consulting notes. "It has something to do with Jessica knowing that her sister wouldn't approve of her dating a new guy while Ken somebody is on vacation."

Mr. Wakefield nodded. "That's Jessica all over. How old is this guy?"

"My guess is about twenty. In fact, that was Jessica's guess too."

"And when she's with this guy, is she doing anything I should be worried about?"

"Are you sure you want to know, Ned?"

Mr. Wakefield's eyebrows shot up his forehead. *What kind of a question is that?*

"A realistic one. As far as I know, Jessica isn't involved in anything more than the usual kinds of high school shenanigans. I'd tell you if there was anything dangerous. But I've got teenagers of my own, even if they are living with their mother for the summer. I know this from experience, Ned—sometimes it's better not to know too much about what they're up to."

"All right. I feel like a jerk anyhow, spying on my own daughters. And this guy is probably no different from the other hundred or so that she's been out with in the last year."

"Good. So you don't want me to go ahead and investigate him. That's a relief, Ned. Those kinds of cases make me feel like the scum of the earth."

"I know what you mean. But Jim, you will let me know if she's getting into, uh, anything I should know about?"

"You have my word on it, as a fellow father. But we were talking about the necklace. Do you think you can figure out which twin is missing hers?"

"Eventually. For now, I think I'll leave the necklace in my desk drawer for safekeeping."

"Let me know when you determine whether it's Elizabeth's or Jessica's. It's important."

"I bent over to pick up what I thought was a beach ball someone left behind, under a towel," Winston said at the Beach Disco that night during a break in the music. "But it wasn't a beach ball—it was a guy's head! His friends buried him up to his neck in the sand and he fell asleep!"

Todd and Maria burst into laughter. Elizabeth smiled, but she felt as if she were several thousand miles away—well, twenty-five-hundred miles, to be exact. In her mind, she was standing on the deck of the *Emily Dickinson* with the sunshine warming her shoulders as she helped Ben maneuver the boat into a lush, romantic cove of a remote Hawaiian island.

"Ah, yes," Winston said. "It was another danger-filled day in the life of a coastal enhancement engineer."

Maria slipped her arm around him. "Face it, Win. The most dangerous thing you face on the job is a bad sunburn."

"That's all you know about it. You haven't heard about the little kid who slipped a jellyfish into my swim trunks."

Todd groaned. "Ouch."

Winston leaned back in his seat and took a long swig of his orange soda. "Let me tell you, beach maintenance is about as exciting as life gets."

"That's a pretty depressing statement about life around here," Elizabeth said with a sigh. Immediately she wanted to take back her words; she hadn't intended to speak out loud. Todd glanced at her, concerned.

Winston began another story—something about a teenage girl, a bathing suit, and a dog with a Frisbee. Todd and Maria were laughing immediately. But Elizabeth was having trouble even pretending to be interested.

As exciting as life gets. That pretty much summed up the last sixteen years in Sweet Valley. Winston, Todd, and Maria were three of her favorite people. But now they seemed immature—and as boxed in as she was by the pretty suburban streets and cloudless blue skies of Sweet Valley, California. But why was she the only one who seemed to notice how little it had to offer? In its own way, Sweet Valley was a nice place to live. But *nice* wasn't exhilarating. *Nice* didn't feed her longing for something different, something both meaningful and adventurous. *Where's the romance in my life?*

She glanced at Todd, who was trying to toss pretzels into Winston's open mouth. Elizabeth sighed and turned away.

Romance . . .

Elizabeth imagined Ben in the cozy, wood-paneled cabin of his sailboat. He sat at a built-in desk, writing his novel with a fountain pen by candlelight. Outside the boat, gulls called in the night. And the lights of a tropical shoreline twinkled in the distance.

Suddenly Elizabeth was in the daydream. She stood behind Ben, almost touching him, wearing crisp navy and white. She leaned over his tousled hair to read the page he'd completed in his neat, graceful handwriting. Then his hands moved up her arms. He stood, turning to face her, and his eyes were full of love. Then he kissed her, slowly and deliciously. Under Elizabeth's feet the boat vibrated gently from the ocean's rolling swells.

A voice yanked Elizabeth off the sailboat and back to reality. "Wow! The Droids are loud tonight!" Maria yelled across the table, hands cupped in front of her mouth.

The band had returned from its break and had just started playing "Come Away with Me," the latest composition by lead singer Dana Larson.

Todd leaned toward Elizabeth and asked her to dance. Elizabeth exhaled slowly. Then she pasted a smile on her face and rose from her chair. "Sure. Why not?"

Jessica stood in the kitchen late that night, her face chilled by a blast of icy air from the freezer. The tile floor was cold and smooth under her bare feet. "Rocky road or jamocha fudge ribbon?" she asked herself aloud.

"Elizabeth?" came a deep voice from the stairs.

For a split second Jessica wondered if Mr. Jenkins was calling her. *Obviously I've been working too much,* she thought a moment later. She had gotten so used to being called Elizabeth that she wanted to reply every time someone talked to her twin. "No, Dad! It's me. Liz isn't home from the Beach Disco yet."

Ned wandered into the kitchen, his forehead wrinkled with concern. "She said she'd be home by midnight."

Jessica rolled her eyes. "I wouldn't worry if I were you. This is Elizabeth we're talking about, remember? Her idea of living it up is ordering ketchup to go with her fries. I can't believe Ms. Perfect would come home late—especially when she's out with Mr. Responsible."

"Well, they're not exactly late," her father admitted, checking his watch. "It's only ten minutes to twelve."

"See what I mean? And I bet that's Todd's car I hear pulling up outside. You want some ice cream? I can't decide between rocky road and jamocha fudge ribbon."

"No, thanks. I think I'll go to bed."

"Oh, I see. You want to pretend you weren't waiting up for her."

"I wasn't waiting up for her," he said quickly. "I, um, had some briefs to review."

"Right. And you always prowl up and down the stairs while you're going over briefs. Are you sure you don't want some ice cream?"

"I'm sure. And don't leave the freezer door open all night."

"Good night and sweet dreams to you too!"

Elizabeth entered the kitchen a minute later. "Oh, hi, Jess. I thought I saw a light on in here." She hesitated. "You didn't hear anything outside a minute ago, did you?"

Jessica shook her head. "Just Todd's car and your voices on the front step. What should I have been listening for—kissing noises?"

"No! I just thought I heard a noise from around the back of the house." She parted the curtains and glanced out the window. "But I don't see anything out there now."

Jessica shrugged. "Must have been a squirrel or something."

"I guess it must have been."

"Hey!" Jessica said suddenly, noticing the low-cut fuchsia blouse Elizabeth was wearing. "That's *my* blouse! Since when do you borrow my clothes? Especially sexy ones."

"I know," Elizabeth said with a sigh. "It's not my usual style. I figured you wouldn't mind, since you're the one who's been telling me I need more adventure in my life."

"But you didn't even ask!"

"So? You're always borrowing my things."

"OK, I can be generous. But remember this when I want to wear that funky new vest you bought. So did the blouse work?"

Elizabeth shrugged. "Not really. It seemed to catch Todd's eye at first. But then he said I didn't need to dress that way to impress him. He likes me just the way I've always been."

"He would."

Elizabeth looked as if she wasn't sure whether to take Jessica's comment as an insult or a show of support. She opted for changing the subject. "What're you doing, anyway?"

"I'm trying to decide between rocky road and jamocha fudge ribbon. Want to help?"

"I'll help eat it. But I'm too tired for a hard decision like that."

"Me too," Jessica agreed. "Let's have both."

A few minutes later the twins were sitting at the table, eating ice cream. "Except for Todd's lack of fashion sense," Jessica began, "how was your date?"

"The same as always," Elizabeth replied. "The Beach Disco doesn't change much."

"But the Droids were playing there tonight," Jessica pointed out. "I'd have gone myself, but I was too tired." *Breaking into empty school buildings can be hard work,* she thought with a chuckle.

"What's so funny?" Elizabeth asked.

"Nothing."

"Then why did you laugh?"

Jessica shrugged. "I didn't laugh."

"Yes, you did."

"Did I? I guess I was thinking about Dad," Jessica lied. "Do you know that he was down here not five minutes ago, all frantic because you weren't home yet?"

"I wish I'd been doing something exciting enough so that I wanted to stay out late." She looked away. "I'm afraid my summer of being impetuous isn't working out that way."

124

"I'm not so sure," Jessica said suspiciously. "You weren't very convincing at dinner tonight when you told Dad you hadn't met anyone unusual lately." Jessica's comment was a shot in the dark, but it seemed that she'd hit her target. She was sure she saw fear spring into her sister's eyes.

"Do you think he suspected anything?" Elizabeth asked.

"Dad? He's a guy, remember? That means he's got zero intuition. Your identical twin, on the other hand—"

Elizabeth's eyes went blank. "Your twin radar is picking up my wishful thinking. I only *want* something unusual to happen. You know how bored I've been."

Jessica licked a drop of jamocha fudge ribbon off her spoon. "You never told me about that mysterious break you took from work this morning. Where were you?"

"Oh, nowhere special. I was just going crazy in the café. Mr. Jenkins was ordering me around, and the customers wanted their food yesterday. I had to get outside and walk along the docks for a few minutes, that's all."

Jessica raised her eyebrows. "Then why did you look so happy when you came back to work?"

"I guess the fresh air did the trick," Elizabeth said, staring at her ice cream. "The weather was great; the sky was blue. You know how it is."

"No, I'm not sure that I do."

Elizabeth sighed and looked straight at her. "To

tell you the truth, I spent the whole morning obsessing about Todd."

"Gag me. True love can be really sickening. I've never thought of you as the mooning-around-because-you're-separated-for-eight-hours type."

"Not obsessing that way," Elizabeth explained quickly. "Just the opposite. All this talk of wanting more excitement has made me wonder if Todd and I are right for each other after all."

Jessica's mouth dropped open. "Are you serious?"

"I don't know. I still love Todd, I think. But lately I want something more."

"I can see why. He can be even more of a goody two shoes than you."

Elizabeth scowled. "That's not what I mean! It's just that sometimes he seems so small town and unworldly. I wonder if he's holding me back. Maybe I shouldn't be tied down to someone like him at this point in my life."

"That's exactly what I've been trying to tell you!" Jessica exclaimed. "You need to meet new people. So what happened on your walk on the docks that made you happy the rest of the day? Did you decide to dump Todd?"

"*No!*" Elizabeth looked shocked. "I mean—sure, I thought about it. But not really seriously. Oh, I don't know. I guess I didn't come to any decision at all. I'm more confused than ever."

Jessica crossed her arms in front of her. "You still haven't told me why you were so happy after your walk."

"Yes, I have. It was the fresh air and the sunshine. But speaking of taking breaks from work, you told me that you and Lila were going to a fashion show at three o'clock this afternoon."

Jessica gulped. Once again, she considered telling Elizabeth about Scott. But after the disastrous experience she had with Jeremy Randall, Elizabeth wouldn't approve of her dating another older man— especially behind Ken's back. *Besides, Liz is so uptight about always following rules; she'd have a fit if I told her we broke into the school.*

"We did go to a fashion show," Jessica insisted. "It was at the mall."

"Then why did Enid see Lila on the beach right around that time?"

"Enid must have just *thought* she saw Lila. Everyone looks the same when you're sitting way up in one of those lifeguard chairs with the sun in your eyes."

"Enid wasn't up in the lifeguard chair when she saw Lila. She was walking by the concession stand when Lila was getting a soda, just after three o'clock."

"Oh, that explains it! You said *three* o'clock. It turned out that I had the time wrong for the fashion show. It didn't start until later."

"Why don't I believe you?"

Jessica shrugged. "You know how rotten I am at keeping track of times. Lila had said to meet her at the mall at four, and I got mixed up and thought it was three. I don't remember what time she finally made it to the mall, but the fashion show was great.

I'm dying to buy this cute red miniskirt I saw."

Elizabeth opened her mouth as if to protest, but Jessica plunged on. This might be her only opportunity to get Elizabeth to agree to work part of a shift for her, just in case she had another chance to see Scott during the work day.

"Speaking of shopping, I may need you to cover for me at work again. Lila finally agreed that yellow isn't a good color for her. She wants me to help her pick out another new bathing suit."

"I can see why," Elizabeth said wryly. "She probably only has eight or nine to choose from. But I know the way you and Lila shop together. You won't be able to help her pick something out without buying things for yourself, too. And you can't afford to go crazy at Lisette's the way Lila can."

"I know. I should've been born rich, like Li. But I just have to have that skirt, to match my new sandals. Luckily I'll be able to buy it at the end of the week— as soon as I win the tip contest."

"No way! *I'm* going to win the tip contest. Face it, Jessica. I'm a better waitress than you any day."

Jessica tossed her hair. "You might be better than me at remembering people's orders," she admitted. "But everyone knows the most important part of customer service isn't the picky little details. It's all a matter of style. And when it comes to style, nobody stands a chance against me."

"Huh." Elizabeth looked away from her, and Jessica thought once again that her sister was hiding something. "OK, I'll consider covering for you. But only if you cover for me when I need you to," Elizabeth concluded.

"Why? What do you have to do that's more important than collecting tips?"

Elizabeth jumped up suddenly. "Did you see that?"

"Did I see what?"

"I'm not sure. Some sort of shadow outside the window."

"The Shadow knows!" Jessica sang, melodramatically but off key.

"I'm serious, Jess! And I could've sworn I heard another noise."

"You're getting as paranoid as Dad," Jessica said. "Steven was saying last week that the tree by the window needs trimming. I bet a branch just brushed against the glass."

Elizabeth glanced toward the window again. Finally she shrugged and sat down with a sigh. "I think all Dad's talk about being extra careful is putting me on edge. I'm sure there's nothing out there to be afraid of."

Chapter 10

The morning sun felt good on the back of John Marin's neck. There was nothing like ten years behind bars to make a man appreciate the simple things in life—things like the warmth of the sun, the curve of a woman's leg, and the sweetness of revenge.

Alice Wakefield certainly had a great pair of legs, he decided. He was ogling Wakefield's wife from a crouching position behind a row of large crates at the mansion Mrs. Wakefield was working on. *She ought to get herself one of those miniskirts that Jessica likes so much.* He nodded slightly, imagining.

Above Marin arched the incomplete metal frame of a greenhouse-style breakfast nook that was being created out of an old porch. The glass panes weren't set in place yet, so it had been easy to slip through the metal framework to watch her at work on the kitchen.

Mrs. Wakefield's hair gleamed gold in the sunlight

as she leaned over a crate, a young carpenter standing beside her. She carefully tore at the cardboard. "See what I mean, Frank?" she said, raising her voice to be heard over the buzz of a floor-sanding machine that was running in another part of the house. "These new kitchen cabinets are hickory, with an ivory finish. Look how light the color is. The stain on the moldings you brought is cherry. It's much too dark."

The carpenter nodded. "Yep, you're absolutely right, ma'am. I guess someone back at the shop screwed up."

Mrs. Wakefield sighed. "I really need these moldings today," she said. "I may have to fly up to Oakland in the morning to meet with the architect, and I'd like to make sure everything's in place before then."

"Don't worry. Somebody must have loaded the wrong moldings onto my truck. I'll head back there now and bring you the light-colored ones."

The carpenter left, and Mrs. Wakefield was alone. Marin couldn't help but notice how vulnerable the slender blond woman seemed as she stepped carefully across the floor, which was strewn with old plumbing fixtures and scraps of wood. Marin knew that Wakefield's wife was close to forty, but she looked at least ten years younger than that. And with her blond hair and blue eyes, she could almost be mistaken for one of her twin daughters.

Mrs. Wakefield whistled a Broadway show tune as she pulled some papers out of a portfolio. Then she sat at a makeshift table that was set up over two sawhorses. Pencil in hand, she studied the plans, glancing up now and then to compare the design on the paper with the architecture of the room around her.

Carefully Marin pulled out his Polaroid camera. He turned off the flash; luckily he wouldn't need it. Bright patches of sunlight checkered the kitchen, streaming through the greenhouse addition and the high skylight directly over his subject's head. She sat facing Marin, but she was too intent on her work to notice as he snapped several photographs. The buzz of the power sander upstairs covered the clicking of his camera.

Marin caught his breath when she raised her eyes to inspect the skylight. The sight of her bare, unprotected neck was tempting. He imagined tightening his hands around that neck, feeling the tendons under her warm, tanned skin and the vibrations of her vocal cords as she tried to scream.

No. It was too easy. Wakefield's pain would be over all too quickly. For now, Marin decided, he would concentrate on the daughters, as he'd planned. That was what he'd been leading up to all week. It was what Wakefield was expecting. Why waste all that amusing terror? After the twins were dead, there would be plenty of time for Marin to have his fun with this particular member of the Wakefield family.

Thursday night, a clean-cut young couple in polo shirts and white shorts stepped into the Marina Café. It had been a busy day, and Elizabeth was tired. But a tip was a tip. And these two looked as if they could afford a big one. So she smiled broadly and reached for two menus.

Suddenly a turquoise flash whisked between herself and the new customers.

"Wouldn't you like to sit over here by the window?" Jessica asked the couple, gesturing toward a table in her section. Both the man and the woman did a double take, looking from one identical twin to the other. Without giving them time to reply, Jessica grabbed the menus in Elizabeth's outstretched hand and led the customers to table nine.

"You jerk!" Elizabeth hissed into Jessica's ear as she passed her a minute later. "They were *my* customers! I saw them first. You're turning into a tip thief!"

Jessica smiled. "Tip thief? Well, yes, I did seat them in my section. But it had nothing to do with tips."

"Oh, sure," Elizabeth said as they walked across the room together. All day she had wished business would slow down a little. But now there were only two tables occupied. She hated to just sit around doing nothing.

Jessica grinned. "I was just providing excellent customer service, like Mr. Jenkins said. That couple really will have a better view from table nine."

"It's my own fault," Elizabeth said as they reached the counter. "I should have been faster. But I'm exhausted! What about you? Why are you so energetic?"

Jessica grabbed two bottles of mineral water.

"Because I'm looking forward to tonight."

"Why? What happens tonight?"

Jessica shrugged. "Who knows?"

Elizabeth opened her mouth to question her further, but Jessica took off for table nine with the mineral water.

Mr. Jenkins emerged from the kitchen. "Elizabeth," he said. Elizabeth had become so accustomed to being called Jessica that she almost forgot to look up. Then she realized that he really was talking to her.

"I have a job that I especially want you to take care of," he continued. Elizabeth's heart sank. She knew she didn't have the energy for one of Mr. Jenkins's special jobs. But her boss didn't seem to notice her lack of enthusiasm. "Now that the dining room isn't busy anymore, I need you to mix the special herb blend into the house salad dressing. It's all set up in the back—"

"Uh, Mr. Jenkins," Elizabeth interrupted. "I'm not Elizabeth. I'm Jessica."

"Oh!" he said, surprised. "I see. And where is your sister?"

Elizabeth pointed to table nine, where Jessica was taking orders.

"Ah. Thank you, Jessica."

Elizabeth burst into muffled laughter as Mr. Jenkins rushed toward her sister, intent on salad dressing.

"Way to go, Wakefield!" Elizabeth turned to see Jane standing near the kitchen door. The older waitress somehow managed to give Elizabeth a high five, although she was carrying a tray of sandwiches.

They watched, amused, as Jessica finished taking the order and trudged back to the storage room to make salad dressing.

"That was smooth," Jane said. "I didn't know you had it in you."

Elizabeth felt a little guilty, but she decided she could live with the guilt a lot better than she could live with mixing five gallons of salad dressing.

"It serves her right," Elizabeth decided. "Jessica just stole those two customers from me."

"All's fair in love and war. And believe me, this tip contest is war. As for love . . ."

Jane gestured with her tray, a mischievous grin on her face. Then she hurried back to the customers. Elizabeth whirled around to look where Jane had pointed. And there was Ben, sitting at the counter.

"Hi, beautiful," he said, his blue eyes crinkling at the corners.

Elizabeth grinned, feeling energetic for the first time in hours. "What'll it be? The usual?"

"Forget the iced coffee. I have a better idea. Let me show you my boat."

Elizabeth's heart skipped a beat. "You're kidding."

"Would I kid about a thing like that?"

"I can't go," Elizabeth said, checking her watch. "My shift doesn't end for another hour."

"That is a problem, isn't it? Who'll handle this standing-room-only crowd in the dining room?" He gestured around the restaurant. At table nine,

Jessica's customers sat drinking their mineral water, talking quietly. At table one, Jane was serving sandwiches to a family with three sunburned children. The other tables were empty. The fourth waitress on duty was sitting at the end of the counter, sipping a soda.

Elizabeth laughed. "I see what you mean."

"Come on, Liz. I bet you've always wished you could have known Emily Dickinson. Now's your chance. Your boss won't even miss you."

Elizabeth untied her apron. "I'll ask Jane to cover for me."

Jessica rinsed her hands in the sink behind the counter. "Yuck! I'll never eat salad again. That herb stuff we put in the house dressing smells like my brother's stinky gym socks."

Jane laughed. "At least you're off the hook for a while. Mr. Jenkins is very methodical about choosing people to mix salad dressing. Your turn won't come again for at least a week."

Jessica glanced around the dining room. In one corner the preppie people were eating their quiche. And at one of Jane's tables three noisy children were breaking potato chips into tiny slivers and grinding them into the carpeting. "I'm sure glad those kids are in your section and not mine! But thanks for taking care of table nine."

"If you want to show your gratitude by splitting the tip—"

"I'm not *that* grateful."

Jane shrugged. "Sorry to say it, honey, but it's not gonna make a bit of difference in the tip contest. I've got the prize in the bag."

"I know you have a lot more experience, but I haven't been doing too badly," Jessica said. "One guy today gave me twenty-five percent!"

"Oh, yeah? And what did he order? Lobster, with appetizers and dessert?"

Jessica shook her head sadly. "No, just a peanut-butter sandwich, like he does every morning."

"Cheer up. You'll do OK in the long run. You do have a couple of advantages over me when it comes to tips," Jane admitted. "Being sixteen and blond gives you and your sister an edge in this job. But I've won the tip contest every year I've been here. And it'll be the same this year. Wait and see."

"Speaking of my sister, where's Liz?"

"She cut out early," Jane said with an amused look. "Something came up."

"Like what?"

Jane shrugged. "What do I know? I only work here."

"Out with it, Jane. My sister's hiding something, and I want to know what it is."

"You'll have to ask her."

Jessica sighed. "It's probably not worth the trouble. After all, this is Elizabeth we're talking about. I bet she just wanted to see her boyfriend."

Jane nodded. "You don't sound as if you approve."

"Todd's a hunk, but he's a boring hunk. I keep telling Liz she needs more excitement in her life."

Jane smiled enigmatically.

"Is there something you're not telling me?"

"Just that she said she'd be back around the end of the shift. If you're not here, she'll assume you caught a ride."

"With my luck I'll be stranded here, while Liz and Todd are out reading Shakespeare or something."

"I wouldn't know about that," Jane said. "But I do know I have to start the inventory of the storage room. Mr. Jenkins is out, and the other waitress went home. Can you handle things in the dining room for a while?"

"Most of it," Jessica said. "But the kids with the potato chips are your problem!"

"OK, OK. I'll be back to check on them in ten minutes. Just give me a shout if they start hurling dishes."

Jessica poured herself an iced tea and sat at the counter. She knew she should be finding something useful and waitress-y to do, like sweeping the floor or wrapping silverware into neat little napkin bundles. But what was the point, when there was no boss around to see her doing it? Sweeping the floor wouldn't make anyone leave her a bigger tip.

A few minutes later the bell on the door jingled. Todd and Winston sauntered into the restaurant, looking considerably more tanned than either of them had been at the beginning of the week.

"Hi, Jessica!" Todd greeted her. "I'm looking for Elizabeth. Is she in the back?"

Jessica's mind raced. So Jane had been lying to

cover for Elizabeth, who was definitely not out with her boyfriend. *Unless Elizabeth has another boyfriend on the side!* It seemed absurd. *Elizabeth?* On the other hand, her twin had seemed fed up with Todd lately, and she claimed she was looking for adventure.

Jessica wondered wickedly if she should say just enough to get Todd worried, to pay Elizabeth back for keeping secrets from her. After a few moments Jessica decided against it. After all, she was keeping secrets too. If Elizabeth learned about Scott, Jessica definitely didn't want her blabbing the truth to everyone.

"No, Todd. Liz isn't in the back. In fact, she isn't here at all. We weren't busy, so Mr. Jenkins told her she could take off an hour early," she lied. "She was looking pretty ragged."

"Is she all right, Jess?" Todd asked, settling himself onto one of the vinyl-covered stools at the counter. Winston took the one next to him. "She's seemed distracted this week."

"She's fine," Jessica assured him. "She's just going through some kind of phase."

"Well, I've thought of a way to cheer her up," Todd said. "We have a date to go out Saturday night, but we hadn't decided exactly where to go. I thought of something I think she'll like a lot. I'm planning to surprise her."

"Oh, yeah?" Jessica asked. "Where are you going to take her? A fancy, sophisticated restaurant?"

Todd shook his head. "Nah. Elizabeth isn't into

that kind of stuff. But she said she wanted to do something different. You know, it's been at least six months since we went bowling!"

Jessica tried not to look too horrified. "*Bowling?* I don't think that's what Elizabeth meant by different."

"I know. That's the beauty of it. It's completely unexpected!"

Winston nodded. "I think it's a great idea. Maybe I should see if Maria wants to come along, and we can join you."

Jessica sighed. "Lucky Maria."

"I don't think so, Win," Todd said. "I want this to be just me and Liz—you know, a really special evening."

Jessica suddenly understood exactly what Elizabeth meant about wanting to meet new people.

"But Jessica, you still haven't said where Elizabeth went," Todd remembered after Jessica had taken their order and was pouring a root beer and an orange soda. "Are you sure she's OK?"

"She's just tired. It's been a hectic day here, believe it or not. Liz thought some fresh air would wake her up. She said she was going to take a walk along the docks and look at the boats."

Todd looked thoughtful. "Maybe I should run out and try to catch her."

Jessica didn't know where Elizabeth was or what she was doing. But if Todd wasn't supposed to find her, it was probably safest for him to stay in the café. "Actually, Todd, I could be wrong about that. She might have said she was going to walk along the beach. I don't remember for sure."

"Synchronize watches!" Winston ordered. "Our mission, if we choose to accept it, is to locate one missing blond waitress. You check the docks, Wilkins, and I'll check the beach. After all, I am a certified coastal enhancement engineer."

Jessica laughed. "You mean beach custodian."

"You wound me."

"No, but somebody should."

"It won't do much good to charge around searching for Liz," Jessica told Todd. "She could have gone anywhere. Besides, she said she'd be back around five o'clock. Why don't you stay here, drink your sodas, and maybe order a snack? I could use another good tip before I get off today."

"Actually, Jessica, I've got a tip for you right now," Winston told her.

"Really?"

"Sure. Are you ready?" He cupped his hand around his mouth and spoke toward her ear in a stage whisper. "Try putting on a clean apron."

"Ha ha. Very funny. Now I'm getting advice on my looks from a guy whose nose is pink and peeling. That's pretty gross."

"Injuries sustained in the line of duty, Jess. No sacrifice is too great for a—"

Jessica and Todd droned in together. "A coastal enhancement engineer!"

"I can't believe it!" Elizabeth exclaimed, gesturing around the wood-paneled cabin of Ben's sailboat. "This is exactly how I pictured it!"

"It's small, but it's home," Ben said.

Elizabeth touched the dark, glossy wood of Ben's built-in desk. "Is this where you write your novel?"

"This is the place," he said, nodding.

Elizabeth scanned the titles of the leather-bound books that lined the walls. "Coleridge's 'Rime of the Ancient Mariner'!" she said. "That's one of my favorite poems. And here are two volumes of Emily Dickinson. And *Moby Dick*. I love that book!"

"And these over here are all Russian," Ben told her. "Tolstoy, Dostoyevsky, and the others. I like a big, complicated plot I can really sink my teeth into. Especially for the long, quiet voyages by myself."

"You have some of my very favorite authors here," Elizabeth said. "It's amazing how we like to read all the same things."

Ben led her up the narrow staircase to the deck of the boat. "I just had a thought. Do you want to go for a sail?"

Elizabeth opened her mouth to say no. After all, Ben was still a stranger—even if he did like poetry. And she had to be back at the café in time to give Jessica a ride home.

"I won't take no for an answer," Ben said. "We'll just go for a quick spin—you'll be back in no time."

Elizabeth hesitated.

"Come on, Liz. It'll be an adventure."

At the word *adventure,* Elizabeth envisioned herself sailing into the picture-postcard harbor she'd been imagining.

"I'd love to go for a sail," she heard herself saying. *And why not?*

A half hour later, she scanned the harbor of her hometown from a quarter mile offshore. "Sweet Valley looks absolutely beautiful from out here!" she marveled. "It's like some Mediterranean village."

"It is lovely," Ben said. But he was staring into her eyes, not at the coastline. Elizabeth felt her face redden.

She turned away from the helm and examined the network of ropes that kept the sails in place. "This is a much bigger boat than the ones I've sailed," she said. "How do you manage it on your own?"

"Oh, it's not too difficult once you get the hang of it," Ben said. "And it's worth every bit of trouble. There's nothing like sailing out on the open sea, with nothing but—"

He grinned, and Elizabeth knew just what he was thinking. She finished the line from 'Rime of the Ancient Mariner' with him. "'Water, water everywhere!'"

"You really do read Coleridge!" Elizabeth said. "I thought maybe you just kept the book around to convince poetry lovers that you're trustworthy."

"Did it work?"

"I'm not sure yet," Elizabeth answered truthfully. "I hope so."

She gazed back at Ben as he leaned over to check an instrument. If anything, he was better looking when he was on his boat. He seemed relaxed and comfortable behind the helm. Even standing still he seemed to be in motion, more alive than anyone she normally saw in sleepy little Sweet Valley. Ben's tanned face looked alert and vital, and his eyes were bluer than the sky.

Those eyes met her own, and he smiled. "You look exactly like the goddess of the sea," he said.

"You've got to be kidding. With my hair blowing all over the place?"

"Especially with your hair blowing around you," he said, his eyes holding hers.

Elizabeth took a few steps closer. She felt mesmerized, imagining what it would feel like to have his arms around her and his lips against hers. *No!* She wouldn't give in to temptation. She had to think of Todd. As long as she and Ben could keep up a conversation, she could stay in control enough not to do anything she might regret.

"Do you often have guests on board?" she asked.

Ben shook his head slowly. "You're the first," he whispered.

Elizabeth smiled dreamily. Again she thought how easy it would be to lose herself in his dark blue eyes. Then she thought of Todd's brown eyes. Elizabeth shook her head and tore her glance away. She was still dating Todd, no matter how bored she was with him lately. And even looking at Ben, this close up, felt dangerous.

Instead Elizabeth strolled to the bow of the boat and let the wind and salt spray wash over her. She took a deep breath. The salt air rushed through her body—cold, fresh, and exhilarating. Elizabeth felt as if she'd been in prison for sixteen years and had just been set free.

"I should have had an adventure a long, long time ago," she said, her voice whipped away instantly by the wind. "Today is the start of a whole new life."

Chapter 11

A block away from the Wakefield house, John Marin chuckled as he watched Mr. Wakefield disappear through the front door on Thursday evening. "That's right, Counselor," he said with a sneer. "The mailbox is empty today. Let's see what that does to your peace of mind."

Marin set the binoculars down on the seat beside him and started up the car. His plan was working better than he had anticipated. Ned Wakefield was out of his mind with fright. And the twins had no idea who he was or how dangerous he could be. He'd been close to both of them several times now—at the restaurant, on his boat, and in the dark auditorium of the empty school building. But he'd used a tremendous amount of self-restraint. If there was one thing he'd learned about in ten years of prison, it was waiting.

He flipped down the window visor with

Wakefield's photograph on it. "The wait won't be for much longer, Ned," he said. "In fact, I've chosen my first twin. As soon as you're as terrified as I want you to be, I'll make my move. But first, how about one more package?"

From the pocket of his jacket he pulled the snapshots he had taken of Mrs. Wakefield at the remodeling site that morning. "Ned, you're a lucky man," he said, smacking his lips. "I had a pretty one of my own once. But she didn't want to wait through a twenty-five-year sentence." He narrowed his eyes. "By the time I finish with your family, you'll know what it's like to be alone too."

He picked out his favorite snapshot—a stray breeze had lifted Mrs. Wakefield's skirt a few inches above her knees. He smiled at the photograph. "Here's one to make hubby cringe, Alice. I'll write a little love note to Ned on the back of this pretty picture." He looked at her legs again. "On second thought, maybe I'll keep that particular photo for myself." Marin shoved the picture back into his pocket and pulled out his second-favorite shot instead. He scrawled a few words on the back, then sealed it in an envelope.

Soon Wakefield might have the police watching his house. So dropping the envelope in the mailbox directly was out of the question. Instead he would mail it from the post office a few blocks away. It would still arrive by Friday.

Marin rubbed his hands together, anticipating his prey's horrified reaction. He could hardly wait.

*   *   *

Mr. Wakefield stalked through the house that evening. There was no mail that day from Marin. Although Mr. Wakefield was glad to be spared further evidence of Marin's proximity to his daughters, the absence of a visible threat set his nerves even more on edge. The silence seemed like the calm before the storm.

Something else had upset him almost as soon as he'd walked into the house. Prince Albert's brown studded collar was missing, though Mr. Wakefield was sure the dog had been wearing it that morning. The implication hit him like a bullet in the chest. Somebody had taken off the dog's collar within the last eight hours. But Prince Albert had been locked in the house all day, alone.

At least, the dog was supposed to have been alone.

Maybe it wasn't Marin, he told himself. It was possible that the collar had slipped off by itself. He'd probably find the strip of leather lying in one of Prince Albert's favorite spots.

But the collar wasn't under the kitchen table or near the living room couch. In fact, it didn't seem to be anywhere downstairs. Upstairs, Mr. Wakefield cautiously reached for the door of Jessica's room. Prince Albert was Jessica's dog more than anyone's, and he seemed to have a special affection for her disorderly bedroom.

Snooping in his daughters' bedrooms wasn't Mr. Wakefield's usual style. He swallowed his guilt and slowly pushed open the door, feeling a sense of rising panic. He almost expected to see Marin sitting on Jessica's unmade bed, a leer on his face.

The room was empty—if any room that was perpetually covered in mounds of laundry, compact disks, and notebooks could be called empty.

If it were anyone else's bedroom, Mr. Wakefield would have been horrified at the sight, convinced that Marin had ransacked the place. But messiness came as naturally to Jessica as flirting with boys and showing up everywhere a half hour late. It was oddly comforting to stand in her room and know that it was the same as ever. Untouched.

"What's that?" he cried suddenly. Prince Albert's dog collar lay neatly in the middle of Jessica's pillow, and a piece of crumpled lavender notebook paper was attached to it. The writing was in Marin's messy scrawl.

You ought to do something about the lock on the kitchen door, Ned, the note said. *You don't want strangers in the house.*

Mr. Wakefield jumped when he heard a voice behind him.

"Hi, honey," Mrs. Wakefield said from the doorway, a puzzled look on her face. "Is there something wrong in here?"

Mr. Wakefield shoved the note into his pocket. "No, nothing at all," he said quickly. "Prince Albert's collar was missing, and I just found it here, by Jessica's bed. I guess it slipped off him during the day."

"That's strange. I didn't know that collar was loose."

Mr. Wakefield kissed his wife, wondering if the time had come to tell her about John Marin. The situation was becoming more and more serious; she had a right to know what was happening. He'd have to tell her all about it after dinner that night.

"How was your day?" he asked as they walked downstairs toward the kitchen. "Is your mansion coming together all right?"

Mrs. Wakefield laughed. "I wish it *was* my mansion! Actually, it's looking great. Except for the finishing work, the new kitchen is almost ready. And speaking of kitchens, how's pasta and pesto sound for dinner? I picked up the sauce on my way home."

"Great," he said, pulling lettuce and tomatoes out of the refrigerator. "I'll make a salad."

"Did you hear from Steven today?"

Mr. Wakefield nodded. "He called the office. Amanda's really pleased with the work he's doing. She wants him to stay at least another week."

"But surely he can come home for the weekend? I thought he was planning to see Billie."

Mr. Wakefield grinned sheepishly. "Actually, I bought him a plane ticket so that Billie could fly up to visit him. It sounded as if they could both use a mini-vacation." In truth, it had seemed like the best way to ensure Steven's safety for the next few days.

"That was sweet of you, Ned. I had no idea you were planning that."

"It was sort of a spur-of-the-moment thing," he lied.

"Well, I have some plans for the weekend that I wanted to tell you about."

"Oh?"

"It just came up today, Ned. The architect in Oakland has some revisions on the plans for the master bedroom, and he wants to go over them in detail. He can't make it down this weekend, so he's asked me to fly up to the bay area for the weekend. I called the airport, and there's a flight at seven in the morning."

Mr. Wakefield tried to keep the relief out of his voice. "So you'll be gone all weekend?"

"Well, I was hoping both of us could go."

"Both of us?" He looked down at the counter, his mind racing.

"Sure. Why don't you come with me? You've been stressed out all week, and we haven't had much of a chance to talk. We can get a hotel room in San Francisco, somewhere romantic. I'll have to work a few hours on Saturday, but besides that, it'll be our own little getaway!"

"That sounds great, Alice. But I don't think we should leave the girls all by themselves."

"They're sixteen years old, Ned. They've been by themselves for a weekend plenty of times! Besides, they've both been working so hard all week that they'll be too tired to get into trouble."

Mr. Wakefield smiled weakly. "You're right, of course. But I still don't feel good about leaving them."

"Sweetheart, they'll be fine."

"It's not just the girls," Mr. Wakefield continued. "It's this wrongful-dismissal suit we're working on. Oilcam is a heavy hitter—they've got us up against the best lawyers on the West Coast. I'm going to have to put in a lot of homework on this one." Mr. Wakefield took his wife's hand. "But I'll tell you what, Alice. In a few weeks, when, uh, *things* have settled down a little, the two of us will go on a romantic weekend together—Tahoe, Napa Valley, Palm Springs, Catalina, anywhere you want."

"That sounds wonderful," she said, ruffling his hair.

Mr. Wakefield rinsed off his hands. "Now, if you've got things under control here in the kitchen, I've got a phone call to make before dinner. I'll be in my den."

A few minutes later Mr. Wakefield sat at his desk, straining his ears for the sound of the girls' Jeep in the driveway. He'd feel a lot better when he saw that they were safely home from another day at work.

"First the Christmas card, then the necklace, and now the dog's collar," he muttered. "Three times constitutes a pattern. Cabrini has to agree that we now have probable cause to pick up Marin, if we can find him."

He slid the elf photograph out of an envelope and tossed it onto the desk, next to the lavender slip of paper he'd found with the dog collar. Then he slid open the top desk drawer, where he'd left the gold lavaliere.

The necklace was gone.

Mr. Wakefield used his fist to pound the desk drawer shut. Nobody in his family would go near his desk drawers. Marin must have taken the necklace back. *He's toying with me again.*

Through the door he heard the clatter of plates as his wife set the table. He sighed, thinking of her. She was still as beautiful as the day they were married, and she'd hardly aged at all in the ten years since Marin's trial. It was comforting to know that she would be safely out of town for the weekend. It also meant that he didn't need to say anything to her about Marin. She'd refuse to go to Oakland if she thought her daughters were in danger.

And they were definitely in danger. Mr. Wakefield had assumed that the girls needed protection only when they were away from the house. But obviously, Marin could get into the Wakefields' home anytime he wanted.

"You don't want strangers in the house," he read aloud from the lavender-colored note. He shuddered, then picked up the telephone and dialed Detective Cabrini at the Sweet Valley police department.

"Tony? It's Ned Wakefield." He waved the note in front of the receiver, as if the police detective could see it through the phone. "This Marin thing has gotten out of hand. I think I've got enough evidence now for you to make a case."

"What have you got?"

"Three threatening notes, and evidence that he's been inside my house at least three times. And I want

153

to report a missing necklace as well. If you can't get him on anything else, maybe you can at least hold him for being in possession of stolen property, if you can find the necklace on him."

"We still haven't been able to locate the guy, Ned. We suspect he's been using several aliases since he left prison. It's making him hard to track."

"Are you saying you can't help me?"

"No, that's not what I'm saying at all," the detective answered quickly. "I think we can prove now that you're being harassed, if nothing else. I can make a case for getting your family some protection. What exactly are you asking for?"

"I want you to assign someone to watch my house, twenty-four hours a day."

"Done," the detective agreed. "I'll have at least one squad car outside your house, starting first thing in the morning. The next time Marin shows up there, he can kiss his freedom good-bye."

"Let me guess," Elizabeth said to her first customer of the day on Friday morning, "I bet you'll have a peanut-butter-and-jelly sandwich and a Diet Coke."

"You remembered," said the man, who was dressed like a yachtsman in a movie.

"It's a memorable order, for first thing in the morning," Elizabeth said, writing it on her pad. "So how much longer are you staying in Sweet Valley—I mean, before you continue your around-the-world sail?"

"I haven't decided yet," the man said. "I haven't stopped anywhere for more than a day or two since I left Portugal. And there certainly seems to be a lot to see here."

"Have you done much sightseeing since you've been in town?"

"Mostly just people watching," he answered. "It's one of my favorite hobbies."

"Well, the marina is certainly a good place for that," Elizabeth said.

"You said it!" He smiled, but something about his expression made Elizabeth uneasy. She wasn't sure why, but this man, with his epaulets and brass buttons, seemed insincere. "For example," he continued, nodding toward Jessica's section. "Take that guy sitting in the far corner, the one with the hat that covers half his face."

Elizabeth shrugged. "What about him?"

"He looks so out of place that I find myself curious. I think I saw him fishing on the docks recently. And wasn't he in here a few days ago? Now I notice that he seems to be watching you—and your twin sister. Is he a friend of yours?"

Again Elizabeth felt uneasy. The yachtsman seemed to be trying hard to appear casual about his questions, but there was a real intensity in his brown eyes. Besides, she wasn't sure if "providing excellent customer service" included gossiping with one customer about another. It didn't feel ethical, somehow. Still, she had to be polite.

"Oh, no! He's not a friend. I mean, I've waited

on him once or twice. He's been in several times this week. But I've never really met him. In fact, he hardly ever says a word, beyond placing his order."

"So you don't know anything about him?"

"Nothing," Elizabeth said.

"Do you have any idea why he would pay so much attention to you and your sister?"

Elizabeth shook her head. "None at all. One of the other waitresses says he must like blondes. Well, if that's all for now, I should get back to the kitchen. I'll bring your sandwich right out."

Elizabeth ran into Jessica in the kitchen a few minutes later. "Jess, you know that customer who looks like a yachtsman, only more so?"

"Sure, the peanut-butter man from Portugal. I notice he sat in your section today instead of mine. The dirtbag probably scared him straight to the far side of the restaurant. I never get any customers when that creep is sitting in my section."

"Has the peanut-butter guy ever said anything that seemed weird to you?" Elizabeth asked as she put two slices of bread on a plate.

Jessica shrugged. "Ordering a peanut-butter sandwich and a soda the first thing in the morning isn't exactly normal."

"I mean besides that."

"Is there something in particular you had in mind? Because if you're just making conversation, I'd really like to take this plate of eggs out to El Creepo, so that he'll eat fast and get away from my tables.

Tomorrow's the last day of the tip contest. I can't afford to lose any more business."

"Never mind," Elizabeth said helplessly. "I was just wondering."

With trembling fingers, Mr. Wakefield tore open the envelope he'd found in the mailbox Friday afternoon. A Polaroid photograph fluttered to the coffee table, facedown.

She's awfully pretty, read Marin's handwriting on the back. *But it's the girls I'm interested in.*

A sense of unreality washed over Mr. Wakefield. He couldn't believe this was happening to his family.

He felt as if his hand was moving in slow motion as he turned over the photograph. His heart stopped when he saw the picture of Mrs. Wakefield, standing in the center of an unfinished kitchen, stacks of tiles at her feet. Thoughtfully she gazed at a blueprint she held in her hands. There must have been a skylight in the ceiling directly above her: soft, warm light shone down on her, highlighting her golden hair.

Mr. Wakefield leaned forward heavily, resting his forehead in his hands. Mrs. Wakefield had left for Oakland—she was safe. But the girls were still here. And so was Marin.

"I don't know how much more of this I can take," he whispered.

Jessica glanced at Scott's profile as he drove them to Miller's Point that night. The night was a little breezy, so the top of the Miata was up. But the warmth she was feeling had nothing to do with the temperature inside the car. The thought of Scott's gorgeous smile and the memory of their interrupted kiss in the school auditorium made her tingle all over. She was looking forward to being somewhere private with him.

"Here's the turn," she murmured. They had reached the road that dead-ended in a wide clearing at the top of a cliff. "And *this* is Miller's Point."

Scott parked in a secluded spot under a pine tree. "So this is where the high school kids go when they want to be alone," he said, turning off the engine.

"See how bright the stars look from up here?" Jessica said, breathlessly. "You can hardly tell where they end and the lights of the valley begin."

"It's beautiful." He brushed a strand of hair away from her face. "I'm sure we'll find a way to use this place in the plot of the miniseries. It seems like a natural place to bring a beautiful girl."

"Then it should be a good spot to, um, do some more research for your miniseries."

Scott flashed her a smile that melted her insides. "That's me," he said softly, "a tireless researcher."

Scott looked into her eyes, and Jessica forgot everything but him. His hand felt warm against the side of her face.

"I have something for you," he said. Jessica was sure he was about to kiss her. Instead he pulled a box from his jacket pocket and handed it to her.

Jessica gasped. "Oh, Scott, a necklace! It's beautiful!" She held up a gold necklace that looked like a long tennis bracelet. Tiny, multicolored gemstones twinkled in the light from the dashboard.

"Not as beautiful as you are. I wanted to thank you for being such a wonderful tour guide."

Scott's arms reached around her shoulders, and Jessica felt delicious heat spreading through her from every point where his skin brushed against her. Slowly his warm lips touched hers. Jessica wrapped her arms around him and pulled him close, feeling a chill of excitement run through her entire body.

Then she screamed.

Chapter 12

Jessica couldn't stop screaming.

"Jess, what's wrong?" Scott asked. "What is it?"

"A face! In the rearview mirror! There was a man out there, looking in at us!" she yelled.

Scott whirled in his seat. "I see him running into the trees! Stay here, Jessica! Lock the doors until I get back."

"Scott, no!"

But Scott was gone, chasing the man into the woods. Jessica locked the doors and hunched over in the front seat, hugging herself and waiting for him to return.

What if he doesn't come back? she asked herself. *What if that awful man hurts him?*

Suddenly she realized just who the man was. It was the creepy guy from the docks, the one who kept coming into the café and following the twins around the dining room with his eyes. *Well, maybe not with his eyes,* she corrected herself. Until tonight, his eyes had always been hidden behind his hat. But it had to be him. It just had to be.

An old movie was on television—a suspenseful thriller that Elizabeth normally would have enjoyed. But even though Gregory Peck had the starring role, she couldn't keep her mind on the screen. She kept thinking of Ben on the deck of the *Emily Dickinson,* with the wind blowing through his light brown hair. She loved the old version of *Cape Fear.* But watching a movie at home with her father wasn't her idea of the adventurous life.

Apparently Elizabeth wasn't the only one who was too preoccupied to pay attention to the television. For someone who was sitting in an easy chair, her father looked curiously ill at ease as she handed him a bowl of popcorn.

"You know, Liz, it's nice spending the evening at home together," he said. His words made the evening warm and cozy, but his tense posture told a different story. "I appreciate the fact that you stayed home on a Friday night to keep your poor old dad company while your mother's in Oakland. It was nice of Todd to let me borrow you for the evening."

"Todd couldn't go out tonight anyway," Elizabeth explained. She wished she hadn't felt so relieved when Todd broke the news to her earlier that day. "His parents asked him to stay home tonight. They're entertaining a client who brought his teenage son along."

"Did anything interesting happen at the marina today?"

Normally Elizabeth and her father felt perfectly comfortable together. Tonight the conversation seemed forced. But Mr. Wakefield obviously needed a distraction from his own thoughts. And, Elizabeth had to admit, so did she.

"Enid told me there was a report of a shark sighting a little farther down the coast," Elizabeth began in a chatty voice. She absentmindedly twirled her gold lavaliere necklace in her fingers. "They closed a marina a few miles down. But the shark was too far away for an alert at Sweet Valley's beaches. It was probably a false alarm anyway. We haven't had a shark near here in ages."

"You never know about sharks," Ned said softly. "They can turn up anywhere, when you least expect it." He sounded as if he were talking to himself. "It's too bad your sister couldn't be with us this evening. I don't get a chance to spend enough time with you girls."

Elizabeth forced a laugh. "You know how she and Lila are! It's like a disease. They're physically incapable of staying home on a Friday night."

"So Jessica's with Lila?" Ned asked, as if he didn't think it was true. "Do you know where she and, uh, *Lila* were planning on going tonight?" He interrupted himself in a louder voice. *"Elizabeth, what's in your hand?"*

"Popcorn. Cheddar cheese flavor." She held out the bowl.

"The other hand!"

Elizabeth looked down to see that she was still fidgeting with her gold lavaliere. "My necklace. It's the one you and Mom bought me and Jessica for our sixteenth birthday. Why?"

He leaned forward in his chair. "Have you been wearing that necklace all week long? You haven't taken it off at all, right? Not even once?"

"No. I've even showered with it on. Dad, what's going on? What's the big deal about my necklace?"

"Nothing," he said with a sigh, leaning back into the cushions of his easy chair. "I just found one of them in the house a couple days ago and forgot to mention it. I was wondering if it was yours or Jessica's."

"It must be Jessica's. Do you want me to give it to her?"

"No! I mean, I don't have it with me right now. I, uh, think I left it in my den. I'll give it to her myself."

"Are you sure you're all right, Dad?"

"I'm fine," he said with a tight smile. "Everything's fine. But Liz, you never told me if you know where Jessica is tonight."

"I think she said something about the Beach Disco. The Droids are there through the weekend."

The phone rang, and they both jumped.

"I'll get it!" Elizabeth and Mr. Wakefield said together. But Elizabeth was faster. She raced into the living room, leaving her father sitting on the edge of his chair, a look of near panic in his eyes. Elizabeth prayed that it would be Ben's voice on the other end of the line. Her father was so jumpy; after a few minutes of talking with him, she felt as if she'd just ridden a roller coaster. Ben's soothing voice and easy conversation would be welcome relief.

Of course, Elizabeth reminded herself, she had no reason to expect that it would be Ben on the phone. In fact, it couldn't be Ben. He didn't even have her phone number.

"Elizabeth, is Jessica there?" Lila spoke in the formal tone of voice she reserved for people she wasn't particularly close to.

Elizabeth stared at the telephone receiver. "On a Friday night? Are you kidding? I thought she was out with you."

As surprised as she was, Elizabeth remembered to keep her voice low so that her father wouldn't hear her from the family room. Whatever game her sister was playing, the least Elizabeth could do was cover for her until she knew more.

Lila sighed. "Jessica was supposed to meet Amy and me at my house so we could drive together to the Beach Disco. We've been waiting for an hour for her to show up!"

"Oh, gosh!" Elizabeth said as realization hit. "I don't know why I didn't see it before!"

"Elizabeth, are you in the same conversation that I'm in?"

"Lila, it all makes sense now! Jessica's been slipping out of the café for unexplained breaks. She leaves work hours early without saying why. And now

164

she's out for the evening, supposedly with you, but you don't know where she is."

"What's your point?"

"The point is that I'm an idiot for not seeing it sooner. This is how Jessica always acts when she's seeing some new guy and doesn't want me to know about it. Level with me, Lila. Is my sister dating somebody else while Ken's away?"

"Now whyever would you think that?"

"Come off it, Lila. We both know Jessica. And I can tell from your voice that you know exactly what I'm talking about."

"Me? I certainly don't know what you mean."

"Yes, you do. Tonight I bet Jessica finagled a date at the last minute, after you'd made plans together. And then she forgot to mention it to you. It's just like her to do something like that. Who's she seeing, Lila?"

"How am I supposed to know who your sister is dating? You're the identical twin, not me. Besides, if I did know—and if it was supposed to be a secret— what kind of friend would I be if I told?"

"We both know Jessica couldn't keep a secret if her life depended on it."

"That's a blinding flash of the obvious."

Elizabeth scowled. "Jessica wouldn't have told me about this guy if she thought I'd disapprove of her seeing someone behind Ken's back. But she would tell you."

"Well, she didn't tell me where she is tonight."

"OK. But I'm right, aren't I? My sister is dating somebody."

"You didn't hear it from me."

After a few more minutes Elizabeth was satisfied that she wasn't going to coax any more information out of Lila. She was a little hurt that her twin sister hadn't confided in her about this new boyfriend, whoever he was. On the other hand, Elizabeth hadn't told Jessica about Ben, either.

"Who was that on the phone?" her father asked as Elizabeth bounded back into the family room a minute later.

"It was Enid," Elizabeth lied. "We were just catching up on the latest gossip. She was telling me again about the shark."

"Did you learn anything interesting?"

"No, just the same old news," Elizabeth said, twirling her necklace again.

At the touch of the gold lavaliere, Elizabeth suddenly felt afraid for her sister. There was no rational reason for her fear. But as identical twins, Elizabeth and Jessica shared a particularly close relationship. And at times one or the other had felt as if she were picking up on the other's emotions, even over a distance. Now a shiver skated down Elizabeth's spine. Wherever her sister was, Elizabeth was suddenly sure of what Jessica was feeling—*terror.*

Tears were running down Jessica's face as she huddled in the front seat of Scott's car. Scott had been gone for an awfully long time, and she was petrified that something had happened to him.

Suddenly a dark figure appeared outside the door. Jessica stifled a scream.

Then she laughed with giddy relief. She fumbled to open the door lock and Scott slid into the driver's seat, panting.

"Scott, what happened? Did you catch him? Did he hurt you? Oh, gosh! That's blood on your hand."

"I'm OK," Scott said between gasps. "My hand's fine. I guess I scraped it against some thornbushes. But I didn't catch the guy. I chased him a long way into the woods. Then I lost him in the trees."

"It was the man from the marina!" Jessica insisted.

Scott's eyes widened. "What man?"

"There's a scruffy guy who hangs around the docks a lot. Sometimes he comes into the café. He watches me." She shuddered. "I always thought he was scary."

Scott turned to her, his eyes blazing. "Are you sure it was him? Think hard, Jessica. Did you get a good look at him?"

"No. I could see through the window that he had brown eyes and needed a shave. But I'm not sure I'd recognize him again."

"You'd recognize him from the marina, wouldn't you?"

"Maybe not," Jessica admitted. "I've never gotten a good look at his face. But it has to be him, Scott! Who else could it be?"

"All I know is that the guy I was chasing was wearing a big coat. And he was holding something soft in his hand. A hat, I think."

"Yes! Yes! He always wears a hat at the marina! That's why I couldn't see his eyes—until tonight, when he took it off. Should we go to the police?"

Scott shrugged. "We can if you want to. But looking in a car window is hardly a crime. I doubt the police would take it seriously. They'd probably assume he was some thrill-seeking Peeping Tom."

Jessica sank back into the leather seat cushion with a sigh. "You're right. Besides, if my father hears about this, he'll chain me to the house until I'm twenty-five. He's incredibly paranoid lately."

Scott smiled. "It looks like tonight he might have had a reason to be. I'm sorry our date got ruined, Jess. But I think you'd better let me take you home. You look pretty rattled."

Jessica sighed. "I am rattled. But Scott, I don't want to wreck your evening too."

"It's not your fault. Besides, I was supposed to meet a guy down at the marina later tonight to give him a couple of things."

"What guy?"

"Just a guy I met last weekend. He's teaching me about the seedier side of town." Scott grinned. "Every television drama has to have its scenes of squalor, you know. I'll just drop you off at home, and then meet him a little earlier than I'd planned."

"It doesn't sound like a fun way to spend a Friday night."

"No, but it's all in the line of duty. Of course I'd rather spend the rest of the evening with you, looking at the stars. But there will be other starlit nights. And the moon is just about full now; it'll be even better in a day or two. Let's plan to do this again in a couple of days—minus the high-speed chase into the woods."

Jessica smiled. "OK. I'll take a rain check."

"I'm counting on it."

Jessica was still a little breathless with fright, but suddenly she laughed. "My dad will have a heart attack when I show up before eleven o'clock on a Friday night! He won't know whether to jump for joy or interrogate me for two hours."

"I'm sure your father will be very glad to have you at home, safe and sound."

Mr. Wakefield chewed his left thumbnail, thinking of the stolen necklace. From what Elizabeth had said, it was clear that the necklace belonged to Jessica.

Marin was close enough to Jessica to take that necklace from around her neck! Mr. Wakefield couldn't keep the thought out of his mind, even with the television blaring in front of him.

It didn't make sense. Mr. Wakefield could think of no logical reason for Marin to steal a necklace, send it to him, and then steal it back again.

Suddenly he froze. "What was that noise?"

"What noise?" Elizabeth asked.

"Outside the house!" *Did Marin have the gall to waltz in while he was at home?*

"Hello! I'm home!" Jessica called from the foyer.

Mr. Wakefield realized he hadn't exhaled in almost a minute.

"Hey, Dad!" Jessica said in a cheerful voice as she

leaned over to kiss him on the forehead. "Hi, Liz." But her grin looked forced, and her hair was disheveled.

Mr. Wakefield's eyes narrowed in concern. "Jessica? Is everything OK? Did something happen tonight?"

"Nothing out of the ordinary," she said, turning to face Elizabeth. "Except that all of this waitressing is beginning to cut into my social life. I was too tired to stay at the Beach Disco past the first set. Once everyone hears that I was home by eleven o'clock on a Friday night, my reputation will be ruined." ·

"Did you have a good time?" Elizabeth asked. "I mean, with Lila and Amy?"

"Yeah. But I should get to bed right now, before I die of exhaustion."

Mr. Wakefield winced at the word *die*.

Jessica had avoided facing him directly since she entered the room. But as she turned to leave, Mr. Wakefield was sure he saw tearstains on her face.

"Elizabeth—" he began after Jessica hurried upstairs.

"I'm sure it's nothing, Dad," Elizabeth said. "Probably just the usual kind of guy trouble. But I'll go talk to her."

He nodded. Elizabeth was probably right. Maybe it was another of the typical adolescent heartaches Jessica was always going through. *Maybe she had an argument with this Scott character that Battaglia mentioned.* Whatever it was, Elizabeth certainly had a much better chance of getting the truth out of her than he did.

As Jessica had done, Elizabeth kissed him lightly on the forehead. Then she climbed the stairs after her sister.

"Jessica, what is it?" Elizabeth asked as she entered her sister's room. "Don't tell me it's nothing. I *know* something happened tonight."

"Nothing happened tonight," Jessica insisted. "Lila and I went to the Beach Disco, and—"

"Save it, Jess. Lila called an hour ago, looking for you."

"Oh."

"Who are you seeing, Jess?"

"Seeing? What do you mean?"

"I mean that you've been sneaking out of work and slipping off on fictitious shopping trips all week. I know you're dating somebody."

Jessica pulled out a bottle of violet polish and began stroking it meticulously onto her fingernails. "Of course I'm dating somebody. I'm dating Ken."

"What happened to 'love the one you're with'?"

"Who is there to be *with* in Sweet Valley? You've been saying it yourself all week. All the glamorous, sophisticated people are from out of town, like the customers in the café."

"Jessica, we're twins. If there's something going on with you, I should know about it. You don't have to keep secrets from me. I promise I won't be judgmental."

"You're a good one to talk about keeping secrets," Jessica said. "I'm not the only one who's been slipping away from work with no explanation."

Elizabeth grimaced. She'd been afraid Jessica would bring that up. "We're not talking about me!"

"Then why don't we?"

"OK, I'll stop prying. You know I'm here for you if you decide you want to talk about it. But please, just tell me this. Did something scare you tonight?"

"What do you mean?" Jessica's eyes were wide and innocent.

"I think you know what I mean," Elizabeth said quietly. "Less than an hour ago, I felt as if you were afraid of something. And when you came in, I could tell that you'd been crying."

"It's not important."

"Jessica, if it's anything that could hurt you, then you have to tell me."

"I swear, Elizabeth. Nobody hurt me. I was scared for a few minutes, but it turned out to be nothing. It was nothing at all."

Mr. Wakefield had to keep himself from rushing upstairs and sticking his ear against the door of Jessica's bedroom. He was desperate to know if Jessica sensed danger. The phone rang, and he leaped from his chair.

"Dad! It's for you!" Elizabeth shouted from upstairs. He sprang to his den to grab the extension there. It was after eleven thirty; a phone call at this hour could only be bad news.

"Ned, it's Jim Battaglia. I've got great news!"

"Hold on a minute. . . . Elizabeth, are you off the extension? . . . All right, Jim. We're alone. What's up? Do you have a new lead?"

"Forget new leads," Battaglia said, practically singing into the phone. "The police have your man in custody!"

Mr. Wakefield laughed with relief. "You're sure? You're serious? Marin's behind bars, where he belongs?"

"Actually, the cops say Marin's been using so many aliases that it could take a day to sort them out and get a positive identification on him. Naturally, the suspect is unwilling to talk. But it's him, Ned."

Mr. Wakefield felt a wave of caution. "Tell me how you know for sure."

"My man at the marina has been posing as a customer at the café where your daughters work. Personally, I think he overdid the yachtsman routine a little; he looked like something out of a bad movie about sailing. Lots of brass buttons and epaulets. But the clothes and the mannerisms did the trick—people assumed he was a rich, eccentric type. He said he was sailing around the world from Portugal."

"Yes, I remember the girls mentioning someone like that. So what did your admiral learn?"

"He did some asking around, and several people at the café pointed out a mysterious guy who's been watching Jessica and Elizabeth constantly, from inside and outside the restaurant. People kept using the word *creepy*."

"Some creep's been watching my daughters, and the girls didn't think it was important enough to mention to me?"

"Calm down, Ned. Your daughters are attractive

girls. They might not have realized that this was different from the kind of surveillance they must be used to from men."

Mr. Wakefield sighed. "I suppose you're right."

"After your talk with Cabrini tonight, the police decided they had enough probable cause to bring the guy in for questioning."

"So Marin's only in for *questioning?*" Mr. Wakefield asked, feeling a sinking sensation in the pit of his stomach. "What do you want to bet they won't be able to charge him with the threats or the break-ins? He'll be free in an hour. All my evidence against him is circumstantial."

Battaglia chuckled. "The gold necklace they found on him sure wasn't circumstantial."

"He had Jessica's necklace on him?"

"So it was Jessica's lavaliere and not Elizabeth's?"

"Yes, I just found out."

"Well, that necklace was the key. It enabled the police to charge him with possession of stolen property. That's enough to hold him while the cops further investigate the harassment, the threats, and the breaking and entering. They think they'll be able to find enough evidence so that the district attorney can make a case for the other charges. Not to mention the fact that he's violated his parole."

Mr. Wakefield jumped up from his chair. "I can be at the police station first thing in the morning to identify the piece of scum!"

"Absolutely not! The defense attorney doesn't

want you anywhere near her client. She says you've got too much history with him."

"But I'm the one with the complaint against him!"

"No, you aren't. You could identify him only as a man who threatened you ten years ago. The police can't charge him with that. You didn't *see* Marin write the threatening notes this week. And you didn't see him break into your house. So you're not a witness to anything. In other words, it's time to sit back and relax."

"How can I relax when—"

"I'm sure you can remember relaxation if you put your mind to it. Personally, I intend to lounge around my house for the next two days, watching movies with my feet up. I suggest you do the same."

Mr. Wakefield frowned. "Are you telling me that my family is out of this from here on?"

"No. I think Cabrini will decide he can make a harassment charge stick, probably in a day or two. When he does, he may want your daughters to come down to identify the suspect as the guy who's been watching them at the marina."

"That means I'll have to tell the twins what's been going on—as soon as the police decide they can make the case. Elizabeth and Jessica will be terrified to know how close they were to this maniac."

"But you knew you couldn't keep it a secret forever. At least the girls don't have to be afraid of Marin anymore."

Chapter 13

*The girls' locker room at Sweet Valley High was dark,
and it smelled like coffee instead of sweat socks. Rock-
and-roll music was playing. Jessica was dancing with
Scott, her bare feet cold against the tile floor.
Suddenly a man's face was staring at them from the
high window. Jessica screamed. . . .*

Scott and the locker room disappeared, and
Jessica sat up in bed, panting. It was Saturday morning. Music blared from her clock radio, and the smell
of coffee drifted up from the kitchen.

"Man! What a crazy dream!" Jessica gasped, not
sure whether she should be frightened or amused. "I
didn't even know I'd fallen asleep."

For most of the night Jessica had lain awake, remembering a pair of vacant brown eyes staring at her
through the back window of Scott's car. But now it
was morning, and all she could see through her bed-

room window was bright yellow sunlight. Jessica stretched and tried to gather her sleepy thoughts.

She came fully awake when she caught sight of the clock. "Oh, my gosh! It's nine thirty! I'm late for work!"

She leaped out of bed and nearly tripped on a pile of purple notebooks that cascaded across the floor at the touch of her bare foot.

"Elizabeth!" she called in the direction of the bathroom that separated the twins' rooms. Of course there was no answer. Elizabeth had already been at work for an hour—collecting all the breakfast tips.

"Shoot!" she said, reaching for her rumpled khaki shorts. "The tip contest ends today, and I'm missing my last chance for breakfast tips. Why didn't Elizabeth wake me up? It's not fair!"

"It's not fair!" Elizabeth complained to Jane as they both reached for the coffeepot behind the counter at the café. "Of course you're ahead of the rest of us on tips. You've been doing this for years."

Jane grinned. "Sorry, Liz. But that's the way the Danish crumbles. This may be hard to believe, but I was a greenhorn once too. I wasn't always the fastest waitress in the West."

"Who won the tip contest your first year?"

Jane smiled. "I did."

"That's encouraging."

"Don't give up hope yet, kid. You're a quick study. You and your sister have given me some real competition this year."

"Do you think I have even a slight chance of winning?"

Jane shrugged. "Sure. A slight one. Very slight."

"That's it!" Elizabeth said. "You're sounding way too smug about this. I swear I'm going to give you a run for your money."

"You mean Mr. Jenkins's money. But before you hustle over to snag that party of six that's walking in, I think you'll want to take care of this one guy who just sat down at the counter."

"Oh, no!" Elizabeth began. "You're not going to give me one measly little customer while you grab six—"

She turned around and stopped midsentence. The single customer was Ben, with the morning sunlight pulling golden highlights from his light brown tousled hair.

"'We watched the ocean and the sky together, under the roof of blue Italian weather,'" he quoted, smiling.

Elizabeth felt the frustrations of the morning slide away, like water under the prow of a sailboat. "Shelley, right?" she asked, recognizing the poetry. "But I think you mean California weather."

"Venice, Waikiki, Sweet Valley—they all have their own unique attractions." He lifted her hand to his lips and kissed it. "I had a great time Thursday afternoon. What do you say we take the boat out again sometime?" he asked in a husky voice. "There's going to be a full moon tonight."

Elizabeth gripped the counter to keep from

swooning. "I've never been for a moonlight sail."

"Then it's about time someone took you for one. I'll meet you on the pier at nine o'clock."

She was so intent on watching Ben's broad shoulders as he walked out of the restaurant that she didn't notice the young man who squeezed by him at the door and moved purposefully toward the counter.

"Who was that?" Todd asked, turning to watch Ben disappear into a crowd of tourists out near the marina.

"No one," Elizabeth said. "Just a customer."

"What time should I pick you up tonight?"

"Pick me up for what?"

Todd grinned. "That's a surprise. But believe me, you're going to love it."

"But Todd, I have plans for tonight."

"*We* have plans for tonight."

Elizabeth's hand flew to her mouth. "Oh, Todd! You're right. I totally forgot."

"So who did you make plans with? Enid? Olivia? Jane? They'll understand. Just tell them I already had dibs on your Saturday night."

"Todd, I can't. It's, uh, my father. I told you how upset he's been. Mom and Steven are away, so I told him I'd do something with him tonight." Elizabeth felt terrible about lying to Todd, but she knew she would feel even worse if she missed a moonlight sail with Ben.

"*Your father?* You're standing me up so you can spend Saturday night with your father?"

"What's so strange about that? I didn't mind last

179

night when you couldn't go out because you were doing a favor for *your* father."

"That's different. I didn't break a date with you to do it."

"I'm sorry, Todd. I told you, I forgot we had plans. And I'm worried about my dad. Besides, I'm working an extra-long shift today—all the way to closing. I'll be too tired to be much fun by the time I'm out of here."

"But Liz—"

"Why don't you and I get together tomorrow instead?" Elizabeth continued. "I've got the whole day off. I know, let's go to brunch!"

Todd shot her a wounded look. "I'm not sure. I have to check my social calendar first." Then he spun around and stomped out of the restaurant.

Elizabeth watched him with a sinking heart.

"Sorry," Jane said, bustling over from the other end of the counter. "I couldn't help overhearing some of that. Are you all right, Liz?"

"I guess so. I just hate to lie to Todd." She began collecting a handful of menus for the table of six. "But I wish he wouldn't act as if I've committed some horrible crime."

"It seems to me that Todd has fallen into the habit of taking you for granted."

Elizabeth stared at her. "You're right. I hadn't thought about it before, but that's exactly what he's doing. Still, I'm not sure I'm doing the right thing."

"What does your gut tell you to do?"

"My gut wants to go sailing with Ben in the moonlight." Elizabeth laughed. "So does the rest of me. You know, Jane, it's exactly the kind of thing I promised myself I would do this summer—meet new people, experience new things, and have un-Elizabeth sorts of adventures."

"Then go for it, kid. Todd loves you. He'll get over it."

Jessica crossed her fingers and stared at Mr. Jenkins, willing him to get on with the announcement of the tip contest winner on Saturday evening.

"I've seen some excellent customer service from all of the serving staff this week," Mr. Jenkins said. He made a sweeping gesture to encompass the waitresses, who sat around him in the storage room. "You all deserve a pat on the back for a job well done."

Jessica mouthed the words with him as he began reciting his favorite speech about the importance of providing excellent customer service. Elizabeth, sitting across from her on an overturned twenty-gallon plastic drum, caught her eye and smiled. Jessica glared at her. *It's your fault if I don't win,* she thought. *You let me oversleep today.*

Elizabeth rolled her eyes and looked away.

"And now, I'd like to announce the recipient of the movie passes, dinner for two, and the fifty-dollar gift certificate," Mr. Jenkins said. He paused for effect. "The winner of this year's tip contest is Jane O'Reilly!"

Jessica kicked the edge of a metal shelving unit, stubbing her toe painfully. She gritted her teeth and tried to smile. In her mind, the beautiful red mini-skirt dissolved in a puff of scarlet smoke.

"But I want to recognize two other waitresses who tied for a close second place," Mr. Jenkins said after presenting Jane with her prizes. "Jessica and Elizabeth Wakefield, congratulations on an outstanding first week."

Jessica smiled, and this time she meant it. The week had been outstanding. Work was mostly kind of fun, a lot of the customers had been cool, and it was nice to be able to see her friends at odd moments throughout the day. Of course, the most outstanding thing about the week was Scott. Through her turquoise polo shirt she fingered the beautiful necklace he'd given her.

Who needed a fifty-dollar gift certificate? If everything went according to plan, in another few weeks she'd be making a fortune for appearing on television. She'd be able to buy a different red mini-skirt for every day of the week.

"Bye, Jane!" Elizabeth called that evening.

Jane turned in the doorway of the restaurant, a dark silhouette against a pink-tinged sky. "Everyone else has left. Are you sure you two are all right, locking up by yourselves? Neither of you has ever closed before."

Jessica shrugged. "Big deal. You already did the money part. I think we can handle putting away the last few things."

"The air conditioning shuts off by itself around

eight o'clock," Jane told them. "So don't panic if you hear a weird noise. Oh, and I forgot to check to see if the back door is locked—"

"Go on, Jane!" Elizabeth interrupted. "We know what to do. Now get out of here! You'll be late for your date at the Beach Disco."

"All right," Jane said. "I'm game if you are!"

"And congratulations again on winning the contest," Elizabeth said. "If it couldn't be us, I'm glad it was you."

After Jane left, Elizabeth turned to Jessica. "You're not still mad at me because *you* overslept this morning, are you?"

"You could've woken me up."

"I told you, I tried to. But you were dead to the world. Besides, I'm tired of being taken for granted," Elizabeth said, thinking of Todd more than Jessica. "You shouldn't always expect that I'll be there whenever you want me to be."

Jessica smiled. "What good is a sister who can keep track of the time if she refuses to pull an occasional shift as a human alarm clock?"

Elizabeth smiled back, relieved that Jessica's anger had subsided. "Human alarm clock, huh? I'm glad I have a second career to fall back on if restaurant work doesn't pan out," she said. "Speaking of restaurant work, we've still got to finish up here tonight. Do you want to take that stack of trays back to the storage room, or would you rather wipe the counter?"

"I'll take the trays. If I touch one more wet

sponge today, my hands will look as red and gross as Winston's sunburned nose."

"Can you go through the kitchen first and make sure the back door is locked?"

"No problem," Jessica said.

Elizabeth grabbed a sponge and watched absent-mindedly as Jessica disappeared through the kitchen door. Suddenly Elizabeth felt a tingling on the back of her neck. *Was that the sound of footsteps?* No, it couldn't be. She and Jessica were the only people left in the restaurant. But Jessica was in the kitchen, and the noise seemed to be coming from the storage room.

Elizabeth decided it wasn't anything to worry about. It was probably just the air-conditioning system cutting off, as Jane had said. She began pushing the sponge around the countertop in wide circles.

Her hand stopped. "There's that sound again!" she whispered. "This time, I'm sure it's footsteps. But whose?"

Jessica balanced her stack of trays against one hip while she locked the kitchen door. Then she hurried across the room and placed her hand on the door to the storage room. She stopped suddenly, hearing something inside. She took a deep breath. It was probably the sound of the air conditioner shutting off. But when she stepped into the cluttered room, she held the door open behind her.

Jessica gazed around the storage room, clutching the round metal trays that she was gripping under her right arm. The room looked the same as ever. Metal shelving units lined the walls, holding an array of restaurant supplies and equipment. Drums of flour, crates of vegetables, and boxes of paper products were stacked in the dimly lit corners of the room. Out of the corner of her eye, she caught the movement of something large and dark. Jessica jumped, the trays clattering together under her arm. But it was only her own shadow, cast by an unshaded lightbulb.

Jessica took a deep breath, but the shadowy room suddenly seemed eerie and unsafe. Of course there was nothing to be afraid of, she told herself. But after the minutes spent alone and terrified in Scott's car the night before, she wasn't taking any chances. She wouldn't venture another step into the room without Elizabeth by her side.

She began backing out through the door when a shadow fell across her face. A man was standing only a few feet away, a dark silhouette against the hanging lightbulb.

Jessica dropped the trays with a metallic clamor as she threw her arms up in front of her face. Then she was paralyzed by the sight of the man's shadow, looming up beside her.

In his hand was a knife.

"Elizabeth!" she screamed.

The knife clattered to the floor. A rough hand shoved Jessica aside, and the man ran past her into the kitchen, heading toward the dining room. A few seconds later she heard the front door slam shut.

✱　✱　✱

"All right, girls," the tall, black-haired police detective said to the twins a half hour later. "I was hoping to wait until we could get hold of your father, but I can't seem to locate him. Do you want to try to pick out the man in a lineup? Or would you feel better if we waited until your father can be here with you?"

Elizabeth smiled at his concern. She turned to Jessica and saw that her sister was calmer now too, after the initial fright of seeing the man with the knife. "We're fine, Detective Cabrini," she said. "We might as well do it now and get it over with."

"Good. Here's how it works. This panel is one-way glass. You can take as long as you need to look at the suspects. But they won't be able to see you."

Elizabeth shook her head. "I'm not sure how much good this will do. He ran by me so fast, right after I heard Jessica scream. I didn't get a good look at him."

"Neither did I, tonight," Jessica admitted. "I mostly saw his shadow. But I'm sure I know who he was. There's this man who hangs out at the marina. He's been watching both of us all week."

"I've seen him too," Elizabeth confirmed. "And I'm sure Jessica's right. He was the same height and build. It had to be the same creepy guy."

The detective nodded. "All right, girls. Here come the suspects. Do you see the man here?"

"Number four," the twins said together instantly. The fourth man from the left was the scruffy, unshaven guy they'd noticed around the marina all week.

The detective seemed surprised. "Are you absolutely sure?"

"That's definitely the man who's been watching us at work," Jessica said. "I'm sure of it."

"Elizabeth?" Detective Cabrini asked.

"Yes, that's him," Elizabeth said. "And it could also be the man I saw running out of the storage room tonight."

The detective sighed, scratching his head. "No, it couldn't be," he said. "We did pick him up near the marina, but not today. That man has been in jail since last night."

Mr. Wakefield was working late at the office on Saturday. He had to make up for all the time he'd lost during the week, worrying about the girls. Now he felt as if he were the one who'd been released from prison. He was free of the fear and anxiety of knowing Marin was out there, stalking his daughters. The twins were safe. Marin was in jail.

The phone rang.

"Ned, this is Tony Cabrini at the police station," the detective began. "I'm afraid you're not going to like what I have to tell you."

A few minutes later the detective had reviewed the events of the evening. Mr. Wakefield felt a wave of panic engulfing him. "I don't understand!" he choked out. "The man you have in custody was caught with Jessica's necklace! How could it not be our guy?"

"This guy has been locked up since yesterday. So

it had to be another man who almost attacked Jessica tonight."

"But Battaglia said the man in custody matched Marin's photograph."

"I can't explain that. I can tell you that your daughters said the scruffy-looking character is definitely the guy who's been watching them all week. But we finally got a positive identification on him, and he's not Marin. He's a vagrant named Pilchard, and not very bright."

"So there's no connection to Marin at all? I don't understand. The necklace—"

"Oh, there's a connection, all right. Pilchard finally talked tonight, after the girls picked him out of the lineup. Pilchard says a man hired him to keep an eye on your daughters, and that this man gave him the gold necklace as part of his payment."

"Marin! So where is he now?"

"I don't know, and I don't think Pilchard knows either. It looks like Marin set his own man up. He had him spy on the girls openly, probably figuring that Battaglia would think Pilchard was Marin."

Mr. Wakefield nodded. "And then Marin framed Pilchard by planting Jessica's missing necklace on him," he said grimly. "So what was Marin himself doing through all this?"

"Hiding in the background, pulling everyone's strings—"

"Especially mine," Mr. Wakefield said.

"And obviously Marin was the man with the knife at the restaurant tonight."

Mr. Wakefield gulped. "Where are my daughters now?"

"They're on their way home," the detective said. "I'm arranging to have your house guarded again."

"Did you tell the girls why?"

"I didn't tell them anything about it. They think the incident at the restaurant tonight was random."

"I wish I'd been there at the police station. The twins must have been terrified."

"They're OK, Ned. They're tough kids. I tried to call you earlier, but I couldn't find you. In the end I couldn't put off the lineup any longer without explaining your involvement in this case to the girls."

"I was doing some research in our legal library," Mr. Wakefield explained. "I thought it was safe for me to work late again."

"Ned, you can't keep the truth from your daughters any longer. They have to know about Marin."

"I know. I'll tell them as soon as I get home. I'm on my way there, as soon as I make one more phone call."

Mr. Wakefield slammed down the phone. Battaglia had Marin's mug shot. But somehow, the private investigator and his hired surveillance man had been duped into identifying the wrong person as Marin. Mr. Wakefield wanted to know how. But the telephone at Jim Battaglia's house rang and rang, with no answer. Mr. Wakefield tried his office number, but the detective's answering service said he was at home. Mr. Wakefield fought down another wave of panic. Battaglia was always reachable. And he'd said he'd be home that night, watching movies.

Mr. Wakefield took a deep breath. There was probably nothing to worry about. But the private investigator's house was on his way home; it wouldn't hurt to stop by and make sure everything was all right. At least he could leave a note, asking Battaglia to call him.

Twenty minutes later Mr. Wakefield stood outside the door of Battaglia's house and raised a fist to knock. Then his mouth dropped open. The door was ajar. His scalp prickled.

"Jim?" he called, stepping inside. He raised his voice to be heard above a television set that was blaring somewhere nearby. "Is anybody home?"

Mr. Wakefield walked into the living room and stopped, shaking his head. Jim Battaglia lay on the floor, a knife handle protruding from his chest. Blood, still wet, soaked his sweatshirt and was seeping into the cream-colored carpeting beneath his body. Nearby a Bette Davis videocassette was playing on the television. Obviously he'd been killed in the last hour or two.

Mr. Wakefield noticed a slip of paper pinned to the collar of Battaglia's shirt. He leaned over to read Marin's now-familiar scrawl.

It's hard to get good help these days. Isn't it, Ned?

Chapter 14

Elizabeth ran along the dock Saturday night, late for her date with Ben. *So much for sailing into the sunset,* she thought. The sun was gone; only a few pinkish streaks remained in the midnight-blue sky. She was relieved to see the *Emily Dickinson* still bobbing in its berth.

"Hi, gorgeous!" Ben shouted. His smile was dazzling in the near dark as he extended a hand to help her aboard.

Elizabeth's foot slipped, and only Ben's steadying arm prevented her from dropping into the dark, glimmering slice of water between the dock and the boat.

"Hey, watch it!" Ben said, pulling her safely aboard. "You wouldn't want to fall in. I hear someone saw a shark yesterday."

"Thanks for the hand," Elizabeth said breathlessly. "But I doubt there really was a shark. We don't get them too often around here. Anyway, I'm sorry I'm so late. You wouldn't believe the night I've had."

"Tell me about it."

Elizabeth opened her mouth to describe the events at the restaurant and the police station, but then shook her head. "No," she decided. "Not right now. I don't even want to think about it. Let's do some sailing!"

A few minutes later the lights of Sweet Valley Marina twinkled off the stern and the salt-scented breeze fanned Elizabeth's face.

"I'm surprised you managed to get out at all," Ben said as she helped him adjust a sail. "It sounds like your father's been pretty overprotective of you and your sister lately. I can't imagine he was excited to hear you were going sailing at night with some guy he's never met."

Elizabeth felt her face turn pink. She was glad it was too dark for Ben to see her blushing. "I didn't exactly tell him I was going sailing with you," she admitted. "In fact, I didn't tell him anything. Luckily Dad was working late when Jessica and I got home. If he'd heard about our evening, he never would have let me leave the house tonight."

Ben sighed. "I hate for you to sneak around behind your father's back, and your sister's. Maybe you should tell them the truth."

"Actually, I did tell Jessica. We had such an intense evening together that keeping secrets seemed—I don't know, trivial. On the way home tonight I just blabbed the whole story about how we met at the café, and about your boat and your book."

It had been a relief to tell Jessica the truth about Ben. But Elizabeth still felt a twinge of guilt for lying to Todd and her father. She shoved aside her guilt. The night was beautiful, the sails billowed like clouds as the boat glided toward the open ocean, and Ben was the most exciting, romantic guy she had ever met.

"It was a good thing I told Jessica the truth," she continued. "I needed her to cover for me tonight. When Dad gets home, she'll tell him I'm out with Todd."

"She's out with Todd," Jessica said, staring from her father to Detective Cabrini. "I don't understand, Dad. We just left the police. Why did you bring them home from work with you?"

"Where did Liz and Todd go?" her father demanded.

"I don't know. The usual places, I guess. What does it matter?"

"I'm afraid it matters a lot," the detective said. He pulled a folder from under his jacket. "A lot of things have been happening this week that you're not aware of, Jessica."

Her father led her into the living room and motioned for her to sit on the couch. "I'm afraid I've been keeping some information from you and your sister—not to mention Steven and your mother—for the past few days." He stopped, as if he wasn't sure what he wanted to say next.

Jessica put her hands on her hips. "Is somebody going to tell me what's going on? Or do we have to play Twenty Questions?"

"You know that I worked in the district attorney's office a long time ago," her father said finally. "It was when you were a little girl."

"Sure. I think I was in first or second grade when you left there. Why?"

"This is serious, Jessica," Detective Cabrini told her. "Ten years ago your father put away a very dangerous man—a kidnapper and murderer named John Marin."

"Lawyers put people in jail all the time. What's this got to do with Liz and me?"

Ned closed his eyes for a second. "When he was convicted, Marin blamed me," he said. "He threatened my family. In particular, he said he would come after you and your sister. Last week they let him out on parole."

Jessica's eyes widened. "Then that was the weird guy who's been watching us all week! He's a murderer?"

"No, he isn't," Cabrini said. "The man you identified in the lineup tonight was paid by Marin to spy on you and your sister. But he wasn't Marin." He pulled a photograph from the folder and handed it to Jessica. "This is Marin."

Jessica sighed, relieved, when she saw the wide grin and handsome features of the man in the photograph. She shook her head. "No, it isn't! That's Scott Maderlake," she said, her hand automatically reaching up to grasp her new necklace. Jessica's eyes widened when she saw the official-looking police identification label in the corner. Detective Cabrini pointed to the name: *John Marin*. Jessica took a deep breath. "Oh, my gosh!"

"You know this man?" her father asked.

"No! I mean, yes. I mean . . . There must be a mistake, Dad. That's a picture of Scott, and he's a great guy. The caption has to be wrong."

Mr. Wakefield shook his head. "I spent a week in court with that man ten years ago," he said, pointing to the photograph. "I don't care what else he's calling himself. That is John Marin."

Jessica squeezed back tears. "Dad, I've been dating him all week! He told me he was an intern for a television production company." Her voice dropped to a whisper. "I really liked him!"

Mr. Wakefield leaned forward and covered his eyes.

"*You* were dating this man?" the detective asked. "Your sister wasn't. Well, that fits, anyway. Your father said the necklace was yours."

"Necklace?" Jessica asked, confused. She hadn't shown her new necklace to anyone, not even Lila.

"Didn't you lose your lavaliere?" her father asked.

"You found my lavaliere? Scott—I mean, *Marin* had it?" Jessica looked from her father to the police detective, horrified. She remembered the touch of Marin's hand on the bare skin of her neck the night before.

Her father nodded, and Jessica gulped. Marin

could have killed her. He'd had every opportunity.

"What about Elizabeth?" the detective asked. "Did she know this Maderlake as well?"

"No," Jessica whispered. "I never told her about him."

"Then Elizabeth is probably fine, Ned," Cabrini said. "Apparently Marin decided to target Jessica first."

"Maybe, but John Marin is a slick character. We can't underestimate him."

"You said that Elizabeth and her boyfriend, Todd, are sensible kids. They're probably in a public place somewhere, having a burger."

Jessica opened her mouth to speak, but before she could say anything, the phone rang. Her father picked it up.

"Todd?" he asked, surprised. "No, Liz isn't here. I thought she was with *you*." He stared at the receiver for a moment and then placed it in the cradle.

"That was Todd, calling for Elizabeth," Mr. Wakefield told them in a quiet voice. "He hung up on me." He stared at Jessica, eyes narrowed.

Jessica grimaced. "Oops," she said. The interruption had given her a chance to catch her breath. Now she felt calmer. She had learned the truth in time; now the police could protect her. Jessica noticed her father's concerned expression and tried to make her voice sound normal. "Todd must have figured out that Elizabeth is seeing somebody else," she explained. "But don't worry, Dad. The police photo is definitely the guy who was *my* secret

boyfriend. Elizabeth has a different one alto-
gether."

Mr. Wakefield's mouth dropped open. "Elizabeth
has a secret boyfriend?"

Jessica shrugged. "This sailor guy she's going out
with sounds completely safe. He's a writer, for
heaven's sake. What could be duller than that?"

"*Sailor?* What is your sister up to?"

"I don't see what the big deal is. That photo is not
Ben what's-his-name, so Elizabeth isn't in any danger."

"Jessica, where is your sister? And who is Ben?"

Jessica sighed. "Elizabeth went sailing with this
Ben guy—he has a boat docked at the marina."

"Did you meet this new boyfriend of hers? What
does he look like?"

"Search me. I never saw him. All Elizabeth said
was that he's a real hunk, and he likes to quote
poems." Jessica rolled her eyes. "I still don't understand why you're having a conniption fit. It's *me* that
Marin was after, not Elizabeth." Her voice broke on
the last sentence.

Mr. Wakefield bit his lip. "Jessica, that might be
true. But the situation is more serious than you think.
There was another murder tonight. The victim's
name was Jim Battaglia. He was a private investigator
I hired to watch you girls. Marin got to him just before I did."

"A murder?" Jessica shook her head, remembering Scott's deep blue eyes and cute smile. "I can't believe that Scott—"

"Believe it," her father cut her off. "And Battaglia's murder wasn't the only one this week. Tony just informed me that a man's body was found today in the woods near Miller's Point. He was murdered last night."

Jessica gasped. "*I* was at Miller's Point last night! *With Scott.*"

Her father's face turned white. "Did you see anything suspicious?"

Jessica nodded as a chilly prickling sensation ran down her back. "A man was looking in the window at us. Scott chased him, but he got away in the woods. I didn't get a good look at the guy."

"Why didn't you say anything last night?" Mr. Wakefield would have continued, but Cabrini pulled another photograph from his folder and handed it to Jessica.

"Jessica, this is a photograph of the man who was murdered last night. We don't have an identification. Was this the man you saw looking in the car window?"

Jessica stared at the familiar face in dismay. Hot tears began sliding down her face. *"Murdered?* I don't know for sure if it was him I saw at Miller's Point," she said between sobs. "But I do know the man in the picture. I was beginning to like him."

"Who is he?" the detective asked gently.

"I don't know his name. He was in the café almost every day this week. He always orders—*ordered*—peanut-butter sandwiches."

"Do you know anything else about him?"

"He was sailing around the world, starting from Portugal. He always wore funny clothes."

Mr. Wakefield stared at her. "Brass buttons and epaulets?"

Jessica raised her eyebrows. "Yes! How did you know? Who is he?"

Her father turned to the detective. "I don't know his name. But it sounds like the man Battaglia hired to keep an eye on the girls."

The detective sighed. "I guess that's what he was trying to do at Miller's Point last night. He just might have saved Jessica's life."

Twenty minutes later Cabrini pulled his unmarked car into a parking space outside the Beach Disco. In the backseat Mr. Wakefield grasped Jessica's hand. "So you're sure that this other waitress can identify the guy Elizabeth is out with tonight?"

Jessica shook her head. Her blue eyes were wide and frightened in her pale face. "Not for sure. But Elizabeth did say she introduced Jane to Ben at the café. So she's our best bet."

"Most likely Elizabeth is fine," Tony assured them. Mr. Wakefield couldn't catch his eye in the rearview mirror. He wondered if Tony was as confident as he sounded. "Still," the detective continued, "we'll all feel better if this Jane O'Reilly can tell us more about Ben and verify that he's not in any of these photographs."

"Well, Jane said she was meeting her date here tonight," Jessica said. "But the Droids sound awfully loud, even from here. We won't be able to talk inside, and you two will stand out like, well, like a couple of cops. I'll run in and bring Jane out."

Mr. Wakefield opened his mouth to protest. He felt sick to his stomach at the thought of letting either of his daughters out of his sight, even for a minute. But at the detective's nod, he let go of Jessica's hand. He watched as she rushed into the noisy, ramshackle building, her hair flying behind her.

A few minutes later Jessica half dragged Jane from the Beach Disco.

"What is this, Jessica? What was so important that you felt compelled to haul me away from the man of my dreams?"

"More like nightmares," Jessica muttered under her breath. Jane's date had been pretty funky looking—long hair and a tattoo. Nevertheless, Jane's smile as they danced had made Jessica suddenly ache for Ken—handsome, solid, and safe. She put her boyfriend out of her mind; Elizabeth's whereabouts were more important now. "Forget it!" she said. "We need you to tell us everything you can about this Ben guy Elizabeth went sailing with tonight."

"Jessica! Your sister wanted to keep that a secret!"

"No more secrets," Detective Cabrini's voice said. A streetlight shone down on him and Ned Wakefield, who stood near Cabrini's gray Accord, their arms folded.

Jane looked from Jessica to the two men. "Jessica, is this some kind of a joke? What's going on?"

"Jane, this is my father, Ned Wakefield, and this is Detective Cabrini of the Sweet Valley police. We need your help. Elizabeth may be in a lot of danger."

"Danger? What do you mean?"

"A convicted murderer with a grudge against Ned has been stalking the twins," Cabrini explained. "He managed to deceive Jessica. We don't know if he got to Elizabeth as well." He turned suddenly to Jessica. "Jessica, do you remember anything unusual happening to you at the restaurant Wednesday morning? Anything frightening?"

Jessica shook her head. "I don't think so."

"I just remembered something Pilchard told me. He's the seedy-looking man Marin hired to watch you girls—the one you identified in the lineup tonight." Jane's eyes grew wider as the detective continued. "Pilchard says he was told to scare one of the twins in a back room of the café so that Marin could come to her rescue and gain her trust. Was that you?"

Jessica shook her head. "It must have been Liz," she whispered. "Oh, no!"

Mr. Wakefield's eyes blazed. "Jane, did you meet this guy, Ben?"

"Yes, I did. And you don't have to worry about Elizabeth. Ben's not the guy you're looking for. He's a sweet kid—clean-cut, kinda preppie, and perfectly harmless. He quotes poetry." She smiled. "He's definitely not the black-leather-and-motorcycles type."

The detective motioned her into the front seat and switched on the overhead light. "I want you to look at this photograph. Take your time, and be absolutely sure before you answer. Is this the man who took Elizabeth sailing tonight?"

Jessica saw him pass Jane the photograph of the man Jessica had known as Scott Maderlake.

Jane nodded. "That's Sailor Boy, all right! I'd recognize those baby blues anywhere!"

"His name is John Marin," Cabrini said quietly.

Jessica's heart plummeted to her feet. Elizabeth was out on the ocean, alone with a maniac.

"I can't believe how perfect this is!" Elizabeth murmured, snuggling against Ben's broad chest as they danced on the deck of the *Emily Dickinson*. "I think I've died and gone to heaven."

Soft guitar music rippled from Ben's stereo system, water lapped gently against the side of the boat, and stars twinkled overhead in a black velvet sky. Elizabeth had never spent a more romantic evening. She gazed up at Ben's handsome face and admired the way the moonlight shot streaks of gold through his light brown hair.

I really have found my soul mate, Elizabeth thought as he leaned forward. When his lips brushed hers in a soft kiss, her heart pounded in her chest. She felt as if she'd been lifted from earth and set on a cloud.

Suddenly the moon and stars were swallowed up in a flood of light that washed over the deck. Elizabeth staggered backward, almost blinded by white-hot lights from just off starboard.

"What the hell—" Ben began in a surprisingly harsh voice.

"Drop your weapon and put your hands up!" boomed a voice through a loudspeaker.

Elizabeth shook her head. "You've made a mistake!" she screamed toward the boat that had pulled alongside. She squinted into the lights. U.S. COAST GUARD was painted across the side of the boat. Ben pulled her toward him, and Elizabeth's mouth dropped open.

A knife glinted in his hand.

Elizabeth looked up into the eyes of her soul mate, and all she saw was hatred.

Chapter 15

A young officer had told Jessica and her father to stay below on the Coast Guard cutter. But through the porthole she saw Marin grab Elizabeth on the deck of the *Emily Dickinson,* anchored nearby. A knife flashed in his hand. Jessica dodged the officer and sprang onto the deck of the cutter. Her father was right behind her.

"Elizabeth!" Jessica screamed. "He wants to kill you!"

A few yards away the sailboat's deck was bathed in white light. Elizabeth and Marin's bodies cast huge, elongated shadows, giving the scene an air of unreality, like a theatrical set. But the knife flashed again, decidedly real. Elizabeth screamed.

"If anyone tries anything, Daddy's little girl is dead!" The voice sounded like Scott's, but it was transformed by evil. He held Elizabeth in front of him, using her body to shield his own. The knife gleamed like a star at Elizabeth's throat. "Ned!" Marin yelled. "I see you over there! Glad you could come watch the fun. How does it feel, Counselor? Was it worth it?"

"Let the girl go, Marin!" came Detective Cabrini's voice. "If you hurt her, you'll never get out of here alive!" Jessica jumped when she heard the click of a rifle being prepared to shoot.

Marin's laugh echoed across the water. "Jessica, it was so nice to see you in the storage room at the restaurant tonight. If you hadn't spotted me and screamed for help, I'd have finished you off right there."

"Let her go, Scott!" Jessica yelled, using the alias out of habit. She knew that everything he had told her about himself was a lie, but part of her mind still rebelled at the idea that sexy, fun Scott was a murderer. She wanted it all to be a mistake. Or a nightmare.

"Don't worry, Jessica! Your sister won't have all the fun. I've got plans for you too. You want to be a star? You'll play the starring role in my *next* murder."

Elizabeth's white slacks gleamed as she stomped, hard, on Marin's foot. Then she grabbed his arm with both hands. For what seemed like an hour they struggled for the knife. Against the network of masts and furled sails above them, their shadows struggled in a deadly dance.

◇   ◇   ◇

Elizabeth broke free of Ben—or whoever he was—and raced toward the back of the sloop. She expected him to follow, but he headed for the port side, away from the Coast Guard cutter. She kicked off her sandals and jumped to the railing, preparing to dive from the stern. For a fraction of a second she remembered Enid's news of a shark sighting. But Ben presented a more immediate danger. As she dove over the railing, she noticed a small dinghy that hung over the port side. Ben leaped into the tiny boat.

Suddenly Elizabeth's foot caught against the brass railing, with a jerk that shuddered through her body. She tumbled, headfirst, toward the gleaming water. Then something slammed into the back of her neck, and Elizabeth blacked out.

Marin was getting away. The Coast Guard boat powered up, and only Jessica seemed to notice that Elizabeth's usually perfect dive had faltered.

"Elizabeth!" she screamed. Then she dove off the side of the boat toward her sister.

Two hours later the twins huddled together on the couch in the Wakefields' living room. Their father wrapped a blanket around their shivering shoulders.

"Dad, I can barely keep my eyes open," Elizabeth said, trying to keep her teeth from chattering. She expected she would have nightmares about Ben—about John Marin—for most of the night. But for now, a hot shower and a warm bed would feel like heaven. And first thing in the morning, she would call Todd and apologize for the way she'd treated him. Suddenly she couldn't think of anything more exciting than a solid, predictable relationship with someone she could trust.

"Sorry, Elizabeth," Detective Cabrini said. "We'll be finished questioning you girls in just a few minutes. Then you can get some sleep."

"Are you sure you're all right, Liz?" her father asked. "I know the Coast Guard doctor said it wasn't a concussion, but we can take you to the emergency room if you think—"

Elizabeth shook her head. "No. I'm fine, thanks to Jessica." She hugged her sister. "I just have a little bit of a headache."

All four of them jumped when the doorbell rang. Cabrini rose to his feet, pulling out his gun. They all knew that Marin was still out there somewhere. He had managed to escape in his motor-powered dinghy. Cabrini motioned the Wakefields to stay put. "I'll handle this."

Elizabeth sighed with relief when he returned to the room a few seconds later with a Coast Guard officer who had been on the cutter. The sparkling white of the woman's uniform reminded Elizabeth of the sails of the *Emily Dickinson*. She closed her eyes, wishing she could put the whole thing out of her mind.

"Are you feeling any better?" the young officer asked, sitting down beside the twins. She was holding something navy blue in her hand.

"I'm OK," Elizabeth said. "Just tired." She yawned, and decided that a shower could wait until morning. For now all she wanted was a warm bed with a soft pillow.

"What's that noise?" the officer asked, rising to her feet.

Cabrini waved a hand. "It's nothing to worry about. I've got a police locksmith in the back, putting a dead bolt on the kitchen door."

"In the middle of the night?"

Cabrini shrugged. "He owed me a favor."

"I should have had that lock changed a lot sooner," Mr. Wakefield admitted. "I didn't want the girls to know there was any danger. But at this point, we're not taking any more chances."

"Who cares about locks?" Jessica exclaimed, echoing Elizabeth's thoughts. *"Did you find Marin?"*

"We found pieces of his damaged dinghy," the woman said. She held up the blue bundle. "And this. Do you recognize it, Elizabeth?"

She unfolded the navy blue fabric. It was part of a man's windbreaker. And the torn edge was stained with blood.

Elizabeth nodded, her eyes wide. "Ben—I mean, *Marin* was wearing it tonight."

"Are you sure?" the police detective asked. "A lot of men wear navy windbreakers."

"I know. But that's definitely his. I recognize that little red-and-gold logo near the shoulder."

"I recognize it too," Jessica piped up. "Scott, uh,

Marin wore it the day we broke into the school."

The police detective stared at her. *"The day you did what?"*

"Uh, can I tell you about it tomorrow?"

Cabrini and her father each gave her a long, hard stare.

Luckily for Jessica, the Coast Guard officer began speaking again. "That's exactly what we thought. If you girls are sure this jacket belonged to Marin, then your problems are over. We haven't recovered the body yet. But the man who was wearing this windbreaker was apparently attacked and killed by sharks about an hour ago. We don't have a forensics match on the blood yet, but that's just a formality. John Marin is dead."

Elizabeth felt her sister shudder at Marin's gruesome ending. She squeezed Jessica's hand. "How horrible," Elizabeth whispered. "But I'm glad he's gone."

Mr. Wakefield watched the twins' backs as they plodded up the stairs, arm in arm. The Coast Guard officer had left, and Cabrini was walking through the downstairs of the house, at Mr. Wakefield's request, making sure every door and window was secure.

"We'll both be sleeping in Elizabeth's room," Jessica called down to her father, her voice unsteady. "So don't worry if you don't see me in my bed."

Mr. Wakefield nodded, wishing he could have spared his daughters so much fear. "Good night, girls. Try to get some sleep."

A few minutes later Tony Cabrini emerged from the kitchen. "Everything looks safe, Ned. The locksmith has gone. Here's the key to your new dead bolt. Every door and window is secure. But I don't know why you're still worried. Marin's dead. He can't harm your daughters anymore."

Mr. Wakefield shook his head. "I know the Coast Guard says so. But something tells me that Marin is still out there. And nearby. I can feel him, Tony."

"I think you've gotten so used to worrying about Marin that you don't know how to break the habit."

"Possibly. Just the same, I don't think I'll sleep tonight."

"Don't do that, Ned. You need your rest. Your daughters are going to need you to be there for them tomorrow, one hundred percent. Look, if it makes you feel any better, I'll hang around until daybreak and watch the place from the outside."

"What about *your* rest?"

The police detective shrugged. "I won't be able to sleep anyway. I've had enough caffeine tonight to float that sailing sloop. And I can read the Coast Guard report in my car just as easily as I can do it sitting at my desk."

Mr. Wakefield bolted the front door behind Cabrini and examined the lock to make sure it was secure. Then he walked from room to room, checking every door and window, as the police detective had done a few minutes earlier. He glanced out the window at Cabrini's Honda Accord, parked at the curb. He sighed as he let the curtain fall. Everything appeared to be secure, but he still felt uneasy. Mr. Wakefield stopped at the bottom of the stairs and listened for the girls' voices. Nothing. They were probably asleep already.

"That's strange," he suddenly said aloud, still facing the stairs. "I haven't seen Prince Albert once since we got home. Where could that dog be?"

"The mutt's in the basement, drugged," said a voice behind him in the living room. "He should wake up in another hour or so—after you and your precious little girls are dead."

Mr. Wakefield turned sharply. John Marin stood a few feet away, grinning evilly. In one hand he gripped a long wooden board, its edges jagged and splintering. "I've been in the basement myself since just before you got home tonight, Counselor," Marin said with a sneer. "Looks like you were a few hours too late in changing that lock on the kitchen door."

Mr. Wakefield clenched his fists. "You—"

Before he could say another word, Marin swung the heavy board. The harsh blow caught Mr. Wakefield across the side of the head, and his skull seemed to explode with the pain. The room spun, crimson, as he fell to the carpet. Then everything went black.

Marin chuckled at the sight of Ned Wakefield lying on his tasteful, off-white carpeting, blood trickling from his temple.

Back on the sloop, Marin had thought it was all over when the Coast Guard arrived with those bright lights. It was a good thing he'd thought to prepare the dinghy, just in case he needed a quick getaway. And the recent shark sighting had provided a perfect escape. Once he reached shore, he'd hacked a hole in the little wooden boat. Then he'd killed a stray cat he found wandering by the docks and smeared its blood on his jacket. After that, all he had to do was tear the jacket and leave the bloody piece with the broken remains of the boat so that the whole mess would look as if it had just washed ashore.

Now he dropped the wooden plank near Wakefield's lifeless body and began stalking up the staircase. As he walked, he slid his knife from its sheath. A board was the perfect weapon to use on Ned Wakefield. But it was too crude a way for such delicate beauties as Elizabeth and Jessica to die. A knife was more elegant. It had style. He eyed its lethal edge and smiled. Then he pushed open the door to Elizabeth's room.

Through the window, moonbeams shone like a spotlight, illuminating the bed where the two girls lay. It was easy to imagine the twins as six years old, as they had been when their father sent Marin to prison. Their faces looked relaxed and innocent— and touchingly young. Ten years had passed, but Elizabeth and Jessica were as vulnerable now as they had been then.

In sleep, the twins were indistinguishable. Two

heads of golden hair glittered. Two mouths breathed deeply. Soon, Marin told himself, the golden hair would be stained with blood; the breathing would be silenced. He flashed the same grin that had captivated them both when he pretended to be Scott and Ben. But this time, he didn't bother to hide the hatred in his eyes. He raised the knife and began to slice down with it, toward the bed.

Something slammed into the side of Marin's body and he flew across the room, the knife clattering on the floor. For an instant Marin caught a glimpse of Ned Wakefield standing grimly in front of his daughters' bed, a trickle of blood sliding down his left temple. Behind him, the twins' eyes were wide in the moonlight.

Then Marin crashed into the glass window on the other side of the room. Sharp, hot pain splintered his body a split second before the sound of shattering glass exploded in his ears. The cool night air seemed to rush upward around him as he fell toward a tiled patio that seemed very far away. Marin braced himself for the impact of his body against the ground, but he was unconscious before he reached it.

Jessica was trembling. She clung to Elizabeth and her father, all three of them still staring at the shattered remains of the window Marin had fallen through.

"Is he dead?" Jessica asked when Detective Cabrini appeared in the doorway of Elizabeth's room.

"No, he's not," the detective told her. "Marin is alive, and I think he'll be OK in a few days. But for now, he's hurt too badly to move."

"You left him alone down there?" Mr. Wakefield asked.

"Don't worry. I've got him handcuffed to my car, just in case. And I called for backup. We'll have an ambulance and more officers here in two minutes. I had to see if you folks needed medical help. Is anyone injured? I saw blood on the floor downstairs."

Elizabeth gasped. Jessica followed her gaze and saw that blood was dripping from their father's temple.

Mr. Wakefield touched the side of his head. "Marin was already in the house when we arrived home earlier. He must have been hiding until you left, Tony."

"Dad!" Jessica wailed. Her father hugged her close.

"It's all right, honey," he assured her. "We're all fine."

"Exactly what happened here?" the detective asked.

Mr. Wakefield took a deep breath. "After you left, Marin sneaked up on me and bashed me with a board. I guess I was out for a minute or two, but it's nothing serious." He smiled weakly at Elizabeth and Jessica. "It's a good thing I'm so hardheaded."

"What's going to happen to Scott—I mean, *Marin*?" Jessica asked.

Mr. Wakefield put his arms around both his daughters. "We don't have to be afraid anymore," he said. Jessica saw tears glistening in his eyes. "John Marin is going back to prison. And this time, he's going to stay there for the rest of his life."

Now that John Marin has been caught, the Wakefields think they're safe. But Marin is out for blood—and no jail cell is going to hold him. Find out the killer's next deadly plot in part two of this explosive two-book Super Thriller, **A Killer On Board.**

Bantam Books in the Sweet Valley High series
Ask your bookseller for the books you have missed

SIGN UP FOR THE
SWEET VALLEY HIGH®
FAN CLUB!

Hey, girls! Get all the gossip on Sweet Valley High's® most popular teenagers when you join our fantastic Fan Club! As a member, you'll get all of this really cool stuff:

- Membership Card with your own personal Fan Club ID number
- A Sweet Valley High® Secret Treasure Box
- Sweet Valley High® Stationery
- Official Fan Club Pencil (for secret note writing!)
- Three Bookmarks
- A "Members Only" Door Hanger
- Two Skeins of J. & P. Coats® Embroidery Floss with flower barrette instruction leaflet
- Two editions of *The Oracle* newsletter
- Plus exclusive Sweet Valley High® product offers, special savings, contests, and much more!

Be the first to find out what Jessica & Elizabeth Wakefield are up to by joining the Sweet Valley High® Fan Club for the one-year membership fee of only $6.25 each for U.S. residents, $8.25 for Canadian residents (U.S. currency). Includes shipping & handling.

Send a check or money order (do not send cash) made payable to "Sweet Valley High® Fan Club" along with this form to:

SWEET VALLEY HIGH® FAN CLUB, BOX 3919-B, SCHAUMBURG, IL 60168-3919

NAME_____
(Please print clearly)

ADDRESS_____

CITY_____ STATE _____ ZIP_____
(Required)

AGE_____ BIRTHDAY_____ /_____ /_____